WIFE

Assa Ray Baker

Raneissa Baker

GOOD 2 GO PUBLISHING

Wife
Written by Assa Ray Baker & Raneissa Baker
Cover Design: Davida Baldwin, Odd Ball Designs
Typesetter: Mychea
ISBN: 978-1-947340-59-6
Copyright © 2020 Good2Go Publishing
Published 2020 by Good2Go Publishing
7311 W. Glass Lane • Laveen, AZ 85339
www.good2gopublishing.com
https://twitter.com/good2gobooks
G2G@good2gopublishing.com
www.facebook.com/good2gopublishing
www.instagram.com/good2gopublishing

PREFACE

THE WORKOUT IN DODGE Correctional's
gym was hot and musty. I had a friendly bet going
on with a couple of youngstas that I worked in the
dish room with before I changed jobs to work in the
dining room. I needed to get away from all the
water. Well, this youngsta bet me that he could out
lift me on the bench press. That wasn't gonna
happen, so I told him to make it light on himself and
tell me what he wanted. The fool said twenty-five
dollars. Really? Hey, that's a lot to some behind

these walls.

"Say, big homie, you up!" the youngsta let out a half howl that snapped me out of my trance. "Whateva you thinkin' about, I hope it has something to do with how you finna pay me this cash after this set, nigga."

"What's my number?" I asked, taking my place on the bench press.

"Shit, I think he done like twenty," my homie Walker told me bef¬ore making his way to get a drink of water in the small, crowded weight room.

"Fuck, that ain't shit. I want thirty, no less than twenty-five, with your bad ass," another slim, loud-mouth youngsta ordered.

"Give me my money, nigga!" said the one I had the bet with, clapping his gloved hands aggress-ively after each word.

I guess that was his way of letting me know he

was serious or some shit. "Thirty? Is that all y'all want? Walk, man, this nigga truly don't know who the fuck he talking to, do he?"

"Nawl, he don't know. You gotta show 'em. Teach these niggas not to play with grown folk," Walker encouraged me.

I looked the wannabe thug in his eyes as I effortlessly lifted the 255 pounds in the air. "I'ma monster! The muthafucka your nightmares are about!" I hammered out the first fifteen reps. "Just call me Kong!" I banged out thirty-five more reps and then got up. "Or you can call me King, like your bitch do, nigga," I boasted after pushing out the total of fifty reps for the young fool and his crew of haters.

I've picked up a few haters since I've been in this soft-ass joint these past few years.

"That's what the fuck I'm talkin' about!" Walker

exclaimed. "Turn up on 'em, Assa! Turn. It. The. Fuck. Up!" he teased them as he took his place on the bench and banged out a hard forty-five reps. Which was damn good for his fifty-four-year-old ass.

I cut the lil nigga's bill in half and told him I'd be by to see him to get my money when we got back on the cell block. Then I finished my workout until the two-hour recreation was over. Walker and my other homie, C.K., made promises to meet up with me in the gym the next day before parting ways with me. I made my way back to my cell block and hung my ID on an open shower to let others know I was getting in it next. Then I rushed down to my cell to grab my shower bag and a change of clothes. Once I was under the hot spray of hard water, I made my mind up to stop procrastinating and tell my story. So back in my cell I made a cold bottle of Kool-Aid, gathered five pencils and a black composition notebook, and got on my bunk to tell it all . . .

What it do to all my people who follow a different path than I do, and As Salaamu Alaikum! to all believers. My name is Ray "Assa" Jones. I'm currently knocking down forty or fifty calendars for an unintentional body I caught. The courts wasn't trying to see it that way and charged me with second-degree intentional homicide, or imperfect self-defense. In my eyes it was live or die. I have family and friends that would rather see me in this maximum security prison than to visit my body six feet deep in a nice pine box. I know many of you may feel some kinda way about the life I ended, but keep reading and see if you feel the same way at the end.

Now please do whatever it is you gotta do to get comfortable as I open myself up to be judged once again.

Bismilla! (in the name of God)

Chapter 1

Release Day

AUGUST 2007 WAS A lovely, hot summer month for me. It was in that month I was released from Pekin Federal Correctional Institution after serving eighty of the eighty-four months I was given on weapons charges. But that's another story I'll be sure to tell you later. Anyways, I wasn't a free man just yet. I still had to sit six months in a halfway house and do three years on paper before I could call myself a free man. I wasn't tripping on that because a lot had changed in the city of Milwaukee in the almost seven years I was away. I needed the time to get reacquainted with my city, family, and friends because people grow and change. I know I had.

As promised, the institution had a Yellow Cab waiting outside the gates to take me to the Greyhound bus station. The officer that escorted me out wished me luck and told me that he didn't want to see me back. I waved and rushed away.

"How you doing, sweety?" asked the white female cab driver. She reminded me of a farmer's wife.

"I'm good, but I'll be a lot better when you get me the fuck away from this hell hole." I answered once I was seated in back.

"Okay, just sit back. I got you." She pulled away, and I didn't look back. Fuck that place! "How long was you in for, if you don't mind me asking?"

"Eighty-four months, give or take."

"Wow, I know you're ready to get you some good lovin' after all that time. I don't think I can go eighty-four days."

I couldn't tell if the backwoods bitch was flirting with me or not, but if she was, I wasn't going. "Yeah, I can't wait to get home to my wife and kids."

"And I bet they can't wait on you to get there." She smiled at me through the rearview mirror.

The wholesome cabbie talked the entire ride to the bus station, and to be honest I didn't mind it one bit. It was nice to speak freely to a female again. Plus I got released from the secure housing unit, also known as the hole. I was there for beating the brakes off a fool who tried to test my thug. I guess he thought I wasn't gonna do shit because I was so close to going home. I hope he can see and think clearly now that the swelling's gone. That incident happened in March. I was originally set to get out in May, but I lost good time behind the fight.

"Well here we are, sweet stuff." She smiled, parking right in front of the entrance. I thanked her and gave her a tip for the ride. "You didn't have to do that. I made good money from them folks at the FCI," she told me, but she didn't try to give it back. "You take care now. And I don't wanna see you in my cab again. At least not coming from that place."

"Insha Allah (if God wills it), I won't," I said, then thanked her again after gathering my big green military-issued duffle bag.

I stopped and bought two nice cold V8 Splashes before boarding the crowded bus. By the route the driver was taking I knew it was going to be a long-ass ride down to Chicago. But it was alright. I met a cute twenty-four-year-old black female on the bus

4

with her young son. I passed most of the time talking to her and playing peek-a-boo with the boy. She was really interested in the books I had written while I was sitting in the S.H.U. and that I was fresh out of prison. I noticed that a few more females were checking me out from afar not knowing if me and ol' girl were a couple or not.

No, I don't think I'm the world's finest man, but I know I'm not far behind either. I'm five foot eleven, with a silky dark complexion, two hundred pounds even, and built like the rap star 50 Cent. I sported a low brush cut and low full beard. I was dressed in fresh dark blue jeans, a simple white T-shirt, and white and light gray Reebok running shoes. It's what the prison gave me to wear home after somebody fucked up and sent the outfit I bought to go home in back to the store. They said it was a mistake. Yeah, right.

When the bus finally made it to the station in Chi-town, I was met there by my uncle Eddie and aunt Amee, who had agreed to come pick me up from there and take me home. I wanted a little extra time to visit my family that I hadn't seen the entire time I was away before I had to report in at the halfway house. We sped down the interstate in their 2007 cream-and-gold Buick Lucerne. It was the smoothest ride I had in years. So this time it was me doing the nonstop talking and asking questions about everything.

"Look, Nephew, I'm happy to see yo ass too, but we can talk when we get back to the Mil. You musta forgot that a nigga needs his driving music to stay focused," my uncle said, cutting off my rambling.

I wasn't mad that he told me to shut up. In fact, I did just what he told me and laid my head back on the soft leather seats. I let the sound of the oldies but goodies fill my mind and take me to a better place. It wasn't long before I was back in the city. My first stop was to see my mother. I really missed her and needed one of her loving hugs. The next stop was my wife's house. I call it her place because I'd never been there before. She had moved there while I was away, so that makes it her home. Anyway, she wasn't there, only my oldest stepson, Bamma. He gave me a big hug and told me that his mother and others had gone to pick me up from the bus station.

After that, I had them drop me on off at the halfway house. I stepped inside and was met at the front desk by a short, light-skinned, older female officer. She introduced herself as Ms. Carrol, with a nice smile. Ms. Carrol gave me the rules of the place as she showed me the four-man room that I was sharing with three others. They weren't there at the time. She said they were all out on passes to home, school, or work. I didn't mind the idea of sharing the room; I was just glad that there wasn't any bunkbeds. The room was set up giving us our own corner of the space.

"Mr. Jones, after you unpack your things, come find me. I got a few papers for you to sign."

I placed my bag on the only unmade bed in the room knowing it was meant for me because all of the other areas were personalized with TVs, radios, and things like that. "How about I follow you now so you can show me where everything is around here?"

"Well, come on, follow me then, Mr. Jones. It's the least I can do since I won a full tank of gas because you showed up," she said with a small giggle.

"Is that so?" I asked, at the same time checking out a slim Native girl dressed in tight jeans and a

8

top that showed off her perky breasts. Oh, I almost forgot to mention that this place was coed. No, we don't share bedrooms with the women. They're housed on the top floor, but we share most of everything else. Before I allowed myself to get lost in the sway of her tight butt, I reminded myself that I was married and planned to do better by my wife this time around. Even though I hadn't seen my wife in almost two-and-a-half years. Donna popped back up in my life about three months ago via mail and phone calls that I was allowed to make twice a week while in the S.H.U. But this is something else I'ma come back to. "A few of us around here like to place bets on who will show up here when they step foot off the Hound, and after that we bet on who will run off once they get here." Ms. Carrol looked over her shoulder at me with that smile of hers before descending the back stairs.

"Hell, I ain't going nowhere, so y'all don't gotta worry about that with me."

"I know. That's why I put my money on you all the way. So don't let me down or I'll find you and put my foot up your you-know-what for making me lose my money," she joked.

After the short tour and signing my life away to the halfway house, I was free to move around on my own, just not off grounds. The first place I went was outside to the courtyard to look through the gate at the block. The federal halfway house was smack dead in the ghetto, on Twenty-fifth and Locust. Just so, you can have a better picture of what I mean when I say ghetto, there was a dope house just one house over from it and one right behind it. Also you can see dope boys and hypes scattered up and down the block, both hustling whatever they had to get what they wanted. I thought it was so stupid for them to be doing what they did close to the feds, but as long as they didn't bother the staff and the residents at the place, they let them be.

I didn't sit out there long because many of the other residents were returning and I wanted to know who I was going to be sharing a room with.

Chapter 2

New Roommates

AFTER I MADE MY bed and put away the few things I owned, the first two of my roommate's walked in staring at me.

"What up? You Jones, right?" one asked cutting me off from the door, or maybe he wasn't, but it's the way I seen it. My point of view came from all of the years I did watching my back in prison.

"You right, that's me. Why?" I prepared myself for whatever. I didn't have many enemies, but then who really knows that? "How you know me?"

"It's cool, dawg. The officer told us you were coming last night. You're related to Pee, right?" asked the one with the stylish braids that called himself Black.

"Nawl, I don't know him," I lied, not knowing if these two were friends or foes of my cousin Phrank. It was rumored that he had snitched on a few of his guys back in 2000 when he caught his case. He got knocked with a large amount of cash and drugs in his self-storage unit.

"Folks, is that your final answer?" asked the other one, who also wore his hair in braids—six of them that fell just below his shoulders. His name was Tee.

I took a few steps back to give myself room to put in work. "That's all I got to say on that subject, and, by the way, I ain't folk's homie." I'd already sized them up. We were all around the same age. Tee was maybe two inches taller than me, but he only weighed like 170 pounds. Black was around five foot nine and about the same weight as his buddy. I knew I could take them if they got on bullshit with me. Besides my weight and strength, I'm very good with my hands and feet.

"It's all love, my nigga, chill. Pee in this room with us. If a nigga got beef with folks, then a muthafucka got beef with us," Black stated, and then excused himself from the room to run after a pretty little white girl that walked past our room.

"That punk bitch got that nigga open. That bitch done fucked and sucked every dick in this bitch," Tee said with a lot of hate in his voice before turning on some music.

"How long will it be before Pee get back?"

"Ain't no tellin'. He could be here any minute

since it's his last day an' shit," he answered, then started rapping along with the Lil Boosie track he was playing.

The song was all new to me. "Hey, what time can we use the phones?" I asked, because I hadn't seen anyone on the bank of pay phones in the downstairs hallway.

"Shit, really anytime you want up until third shift. They like to make you ask because that's when people run off an' shit. Here, you can use my cell."

"Thanks, but I'm good. I don't want my family calling your line back to talk to me. Do they trip on us having cell phones?"

"Only if you got one of them prepay joints because they wanna copy of your bill and your number. These muthafuckas be all in your business on everything. But they don't pat us down like that when we come in, so you can have two phones and they won't know. Most of us do," he explained, getting changed out of his work clothes.

~ ~ ~

Downstairs in the corridor I ran into an OG named Money Bones. He was the man in the hood when I was a kid. The dope game gave him the best of everything: cars, clothes, bling, and women. I was too young to be on his team, but he always showed me love by tossing me a few dollars here and there, right until he got knocked on drug charges along with many other dope men from the '80s. I was surprised he even remembered me from like twenty years ago. We talked for a second and then I promised to get up with him once I got off the phone.

I called Donna, who was upset that she didn't get to surprise me at the bus station, but she promised to come visit me the next day and bring me some food and things. The officer called me over the loudspeaker, so I ended the call and went to see what she wanted. On the way I was stopped by a sexy, thick, dark-skinned girl with a body like Ms. Buffy the Body.

"Hey, is your name Jones?"

"Yep, that's me, but you can call me Assa."

"Okay, Assa. You musta just got here today?"

"Yeah, why, what I do wrong?" I joked.

"Nothing. It's just that you got a visitor and they only do that for the new people during the week."

"Oh, I thought we could have people drop stuff off for us any time before nine o' clock?" I asked as we walked.

"You can. I was just saying that's how I knew you were new. I ain't been here that long myself, but let me go before your girl try to kill you for talking to me," she joked. "Your daughter is pretty."

I looked toward the front desk at who was there to see me. "Thanks, but that's not my girl, just my BM," I corrected her as I watched her booty bounce as she walked away. Man, with pretty muthafuckas like her around it was gonna be hard to stay true.

I greeted my ten-year-old daughter with a big hug and covered her face with kisses. "Pooh, you got so big," I told her sweeping her off her feet into my arms. Ms. Carrol told me I could step out front of the building with them for a few moments, and then they would have to come back on the weekend. Those were the visiting days. My daughter gave me some food and a shaving kit that her mother helped her pick out for me. Peachee and I talked a bit, but not long because her husband was in the car double-parked waiting on them. She slipped me her work number and told me to call her in the morning around ten. This could just be all me, but I could

18

swear ol' Peachee put a little extra switch in her hips as she walked away. I stood and watched them pull off before I went back inside. I heard someone calling my name out the window of a dark blue Lincoln Navigator. I approached it even though I wasn't supposed to get too far from the front door.

"Bro, Moe told me you was getting out soon. When you touch down?"

I saw it was my homie Boss. "Oh, what's good, bro! Hey, pull over and get out. I can't be down here like this," I informed him, looking over my shoulder to see if anybody had noticed I was gone.

Boss parked almost in front of the dope house and walked his fat ass back my way. He was cut off by a nice-looking ghetto redbone chick that walked off of the spot's porch. He must have known her because he said a few quick hushed words to her and then made his way to me.

"I see you riding good. Getting all the hoes an' shit!" We shook hands and hugged. "Bro, you shouldn't park there for too long because that's a spot."

"It's all good, my nigg. Who you think they get their weed from?" he stated proudly.

"Well, since it's like that, hit my hand with some-thing? A nigga accepting all donations."

He pulled out a nice-size wad of cash and peeled off a few bills and handed them to me.

"Here, this should get you by until you get a pass. What do you need?"

"Really, bro? I just touched down a few hours ago. I don't got shit but what you see here." I stuffed the cash in my back pocket. Ms. Carrol peeked her head out of the door and told me I had to come in. I asked her if I could borrow a pen and took down Boss's number. "I'ma call you as soon as I get a pass. I'm not finna talk to you on these lines here."

He gave me a dap and let me go inside.

"Where you know Big Money from?" Ms. Carrol asked, "I don't wanna know. Just stay away from him if you want to stay here like I think you do?"

"I told you I'm not on nothing. I'm not trying to go back to prison no time soon." I took out the piece of paper with a number and then ripped it up into little pieces and tossed it in her trashcan.

"Okay, I believe you." She was all smiles again as she checked over my bag of goodies that my daughter gave me. Satisfied, she allowed me to go on my merry way.

I had it already in my mind that it was best to keep her smiling. I'm pretty good at reading people, and I knew that smile was just a front to mask the wickedness within her.

"I hate that bitch! She always on some shit," said

the dark-skinned girl, reading my mind.

"Boo, don't let her fool you. I see she made you throw away your guy's number."

"Yeah, she made me throw away a number." I flashed her a smile "You know my name, but I don't know yours."

"That's because you didn't ask me for it. You gotta ask for what you want to receive it," she said, openly flirting.

"Sooo are you going to tell me or make me beg for it?"

"Boo, you ain't gotta beg me for nothing unless that's what you're into."

Her words sounded so sexy, and I was really feeling her vibe. Plus I was horny as a muthafucka, I can't lie. But I kept my lust in check. She told me her name was Lashae. "Is it okay for me to call you Shae?"

"Why not, everybody else do. Do you smoke?"

"Nope, but, here, grab you a pack outta the mach-ine and us something to drink." I handed her two fives.

"What do you drink?"

"Any kinda juice is good. I'll meet you in the courtyard in a minute," I told her, then walked back up to my room.

"Cuzo, what up!" Phrank greeted me as soon as I walked in the door.

"Heeey, how you get past me? I was just out front," I said, hugging my family.

"Your ass was on the horn when I came in. Folks told me how you was ready to get down on them about me an' shit. I tried to tell them, but you know what a hard head makes. I had the officer put you in here with my niggas because these other fools in this bitch lame, and I don't want you to jack yourself

23

off for putting your hands on one of them."

"I'm on some chill shit, cuz. I don't wanna do nothing I don't gotta do," I explained putting my bag in the armoire. "So you finna be out of here tonight, huh?"

"Nawl, I gotta wait until morning because Res gotta work a double and can't pick me up until then. You know we done went and got married?" he said proudly.

"Yeah? When that happen?" I was shocked to get that news because he was always known to be a playboy even though his heart belonged to one woman.

"Hell, she did this bit with me. Held her nigga down like she was 'pose to, so I had to give her what she been begging for all these years. Feel me?" His phone started vibrating and he answer-¬ed it. "This her now. You wanna say something to

24

her?"

"Nope, just tell her I said hey and I'll see her in the morning when she come pick you up."

He told her and I went to kick it with Shae in the courtyard. I found her sitting in the dining room/ visiting room talking to the short white girl I knew to be Black's girl, or whatever she was to him. As soon as she noticed me, Shae held up her finger letting me know she needed a moment, then got up and went into the kitchen. I noticed the white girl checking me out, but I wasn't going, for two reasons. I don't do white girls, and I don't want to have to put hands on Black over the bitch. As I watched Shae return with the two Brisk sweet teas, I wondered, Did I fuck up by giving her that lil money and get her thinking she got her a trick or some shit? But looking at her pretty face and body as she moved over to me made me wanna see just how far she willing to go. Broke hoes known for doing something strange for a little change.

"Assa, I know you said you wanted juice, but I got two of these for the price of one," she explained, handing me one of the drinks Then she went in her pocket and tried to give me the change back.

"You keep that." I pushed her hand back to her. "Let's go outside."

"Alright."

I let her lead the way so I could follow that ass. We just chilled and kicked it for what seemed like hours. By the time we parted, I knew she was from Madison, Wisconsin. She did four years for drugs that belonged to her boyfriend at the time. She told me that she relocated here to have a fresh start. I found out who was fucking who and the names of all of the women here. When I returned to my room, I gathered the things I needed, then headed to the bathroom for a shower. It was empty, so I locked the door and took a seat on the hard wood bench. I counted up the money Boss had given me. It was $500, and that brought my cash up to $2,660 with the check they had for me down in the office. I made plans to have Donna go shopping for me some clothes when she came to see me. After the shower, I called it a night and went to bed.

Chapter 3

Visiting Day

DONNA WAS THERE TO visit me as promised. She was looking and smelling good when she hugged me. She didn't kiss me, which made me wonder and take a closer look at things. I noticed that she had put on a little weight, but nothing I couldn't handle. I was kinda disappointed that she didn't bring the kids. I really wanted to see my youngest daughter, Autumn, because she had promised me all of the hugs and kisses I could take.

We found a table in the back of the visiting room away from everybody. That's where Donna came clean, or more like told me what she thought I needed to know about why she fell outta touch with me my last few years inside. Her reason was mostly that a young girl that I had fooled around with before I went in was running around telling anyone that would listen that I was her baby daddy and that I was coming home to be with her when I got out.

"Donna, like I said before I left Pekin, I'ma get you the DNA test results as soon as I can start getting my passes. I don't gotta lie to you about that, and I wouldn't because I want all mine to know each other." I held her hand and stared into her pretty brown eyes as I spoke my truth.

"Bae, to be honest with you, it's hard for me to let that go with the lil bitch throwing her child up in my face every chance she could. So you need to make her stop."

Wow, she pulled that one on a nigga. "How? Donna, I don't know how to get in touch with the bitch, and I ain't trying to."

"I'm just saying, once she finds out you here, she might pop up on you, and if she do, I'ma need you to handle that," she told me, releasing my hand and sitting back in her seat.

I could see she was trying to find the words she needed to say what was on her mind next. "What else?"

"Ray, you say that you can understand that I was with someone else now, but . . ."

"But nothing," I cut her off. "I don't care about that. I told you when I got that time what I expected of you. I knew better than to put something like that on you. Shit, I was more hurt that you let the nigga come between us."

"No, your bitch came between us!" She raised her voice just a little but not enough to draw attention to us.

"I'm not trying to fight with you, Donna." I took her hand back in mine. "You're my wife, and I'm on trying to work on the rest of our life together."

"I hear you talking, but you gotta show me that I'm still who you want. That we're still who you want. I don't want you coming back in my kids' life if you're not sure. That's not fair to them." She was crying now.

"Bae, don't do that. I don't know how to show you that my home is with you and our kids." I could tell from the way the visit was going that I wouldn't be getting none of her good lovin' anytime soon. "Donna, let's use this time I got to do here to get to know each and every bit of one another again, okay?"

"Okay, I'd like that."

"Now, do I gotta change my address to my mother's or your mother's place? It don't make a difference to me."

"If you do that, I'll kill you," she joked, or I hoped she was.

Anyway, she left shortly afterward. Donna promised to bring the kids next time she came, and I walked her to the door. As she was leaving, my sister Sheeka was pulling up in her little blue car.

Sheeka brought her twin girls to see their uncle for the first time. We instantly fell in love with each other. My nieces hugged and kissed me and beat me up like they had known me their whole lives. I loved every moment of it. When the visit was over, I returned to my room.

Phrank had left me his CD Walkman and a few CDs, and Black was getting ready to go on his weekend pass. He gave me a number to a chat line and his prepaid phone to use, talking about it's fun on them lonely nights. Fuck it, why not try it? When I put the phone under my pillow, I found a wad of cash that I knew my cousin had put there for me. But the nigga didn't even leave his number. Oh well.

The rest of my day was uneventful. I found the weight room and worked out on the weights for the first time in months. I was pounding out my last set of eight reps at 345 pounds, when the Native girl, Mandi, I think her name was, started clapping her hands.

"Really? That's all you gonna do is clap when you see a brotha struggling to get that shit up?" I asked once I got up from the bench press.

"What else could I have done besides go get you some help? I'm 105 soaking wet. I can't lift that shit."

We laughed at her honesty. I noticed she was staring at my sweaty, shirtless chest and arms. I wondered if she was turned on by me. "Well I'm done now, so it's all yours."

"Okay, Asa, do you like movies?"

"My name is Assa, and it depends on what kind. Why?"

"I got a few you can come watch in the TV room with me later, if you want."

"Hell, I don't got nothing else to do. What time later?"

"It don't matter. I'm always in there at night. I spend the night in there most of the time when Granny, the old woman I'm in the room with, won't stop snoring."

"Didn't know you could do that." I wondered what she was really on with me, but I'd already told her I was coming, so I guessed I'd find out then.

From there I showered and then spent the rest of the day working on the second book I'd started writing when I was in the SHU before I left the prison. Soon I needed a break, so I went down to the pay phone to call the wife. I tried her three times with no luck. I was calling her cell phone, so I wondered if she was with her boyfriend and couldn't talk to me. With no one else to call that I wanted to talk to anyway, I went back up to my room and dialed up the chat line.

Within the first few minutes I met someone worthy who wanted to talk live with me. I had to send her a voicemail telling her that the battery was low on the phone, so if she was serious about getting to know me she would have to send me her number. She did, and I called her ASAP. Her name was Angel. When she asked about me I told her the truth about where I was, what I was in for, and how long I'd done. Yes, I told her I was married. I explained to her that I didn't believe I was going to end back up with my wife and that I was only looking for a friend to talk to and maybe chill with on my passes. Angel was down with that. All she asked for was that I let her know if or when I worked things out with my wife. Like I said, she was cool as hell. We talked for like two hours and made plans to talk again the next day.

I did some more writing and then went to see what Mandi was up to.

I found her right where she said she would be. I was hungry, so I asked her if she liked pizza. She said she loved it and that it didn't matter what kind. I ordered two, one made just for her and the other for me, because I don't eat pork or chicken. Did I tell you that the halfway house didn't cook for us on the weekends? They gave us free access to the kitchen, but we had to cook for ourselves. That shit was cool, but I didn't want to cook.

When the pizzas got there, Mandi gave some of hers to the officer at the front desk. Her name was Sarah. She was a pretty light-skinned girl with what looked to me to be natural curls in her hair, but who knows these days without running your fingers through it? Anyway, Sarah was one of the third-shift officers. There were two that switched up nights, and they were both cool as hell.

Back in the TV room, Mandi and I watched two all-time hood hits, Paid in Full and Belly. Once Belly ended, tell me why the next DVD she put in was Ray J's sex tape? But what shocked me more was when she took my hand and started sucking on my fingers. I should have left, but that shit right there had me on brick. Remember, it had been a long time since I had any sexual contact. Now she fucked me up when she told me that she didn't fuck or suck the first time around. "Okay then, bitch, why you teasing a nigga then?" is what I wanted to say but didn't.

"You can touch it and feel how bad I want to," she said, wanting me to play with her pussy.

Now I was down to help her get off like that as long as she returned the favor. So I gave in to my lust and made her cum over and over until she came one hard time before falling asleep be-fore doing her part. I felt used and wanted to wake her ass up, but I didn't. I just got up and went and took another shower before going in my room and calling it a night. The funny thing was, I was kinda worried about her telling Shae when she returned from her pass. I don't know why. She wasn't my girl, and I wasn't trying to fuck her either. She was just cool.

Chapter 4

A Job Is a Job

WEEK ONE SUCCESSFULLY completed, things were good between me and Shae. I didn't know if she was told about that mess with Mandi or not, but I wasn't fucking with her anymore anyway, because I heard she burnt Money Bones. She didn't even tell me she had fucked with him. If I fucked her, I would've used a rubber anyway, but still. Punk-ass bitch! Things were moving along well between me and Angel. We talked on the phone daily. Things with my wife were the same. Half of the damn time, I couldn't get her on the phone. I wondered if this was her way of seeing if I wanted her or some dumbass shit. I was getting frustrated with her because I didn't know what she wanted me to do.

That Wednesday, the job coordinator walked into the dining room asking those of us who didn't have jobs if we wanted one. I threw my hand up in the air faster than a crackhead on the run. I still had a few days to go before I was allowed to go out looking for a job on my own, but they waived the time since he really needed someone to fill this position.

I was warned that nobody wanted the job because it was funky and dirty. I didn't care about that mess as long as I was getting out of there to move around every day.

"How much do it pay?"

"The job starts off at $8.50, but if you stay you can get a raise," he answered, pushing the paperwork in front of me.

"Sounds okay to me." I signed the papers. Hell, after working my ass off for 25¢ an hour for almost seven years, the $8.50 felt like I had hit gold. Plus the benefits that came with having a job made it all worth it. I could start getting passes sooner, and my own room. So, hell yeah, I took it.

Like three days after I started the job I started sneaking over to Donna's house every morning before work to talk and get teased by her because she still wasn't giving up the goods, at least not to me. Angel asked me to come by her place before work two days after we met face-to-face. I had stopped by her house coming from taking my state ID picture. I told her that she had to pick me up from the bus stop on Thirty-Fifth Street in the morning because I had like two hours to spare before I had to be at work. Angel only lived about ten minutes from my job, so we made it happen.

This was also our first time seeing each other alone. I was a little more curious than I was nervous because of the phone sex we had the night before. It was just something to do at the time for me, but it clearly was more to her. I saw her black PT Cruiser sitting in the gas station lot way before she noticed me walking up to her car and knocking on her window.

"Hey, you really should pay more attention to your surroundings," I told her, getting into the passenger seat. "I could have someone trying to take the goodies or something."

"But you are someone here to take my goodies," she giggled as she pulled away from the station.

"I've been here. I seen you pull in. I just didn't

come over right away because I wasn't sure it was you until you parked behind the bus stop." I was checking her out as I explained. Angel wasn't the dime she'd made herself out to be, but she was far from ugly. I guess you can say she had a sexy exotic look to her. She was five foot five with long, honey-blonde locks in her hair that blended with her golden complexion perfectly. She had a medium build, but was not fat, and was about ten years my elder. So that put her in her late forties.

"So what do you think?" she asked, pulling over and parking in front of the big two-family home she owned.

"What do I think about what?"

"Am I still what you like, or are you just making a polite booty call?"

"Well, the booty call part is all on you. You picked me up, not the other way around. You're the one that wants some of this fresh-outta-the-pen beef. And, yes, I do plan on giving you every inch of me." I smiled mischievously. "But nothing has changed with me. I still like you. You have the beauty I imagined you would have on the phone."

She smiled hard and kissed me boldly. I allowed it. Fuck it, a nigga been out like a month and Donna was still playing.

"Let's go in the house. You said we only have a little time, right?"

I looked at the clock in the dash. "We still got almost two whole hours before I gotta be at work."

"Yeah, I know, but I wanna feed you a nice breakfast after I drain you." She hopped out of the car.

"Ma, the only thing I have an appetite for is you. Remember I ain't had no pussy in years, so let's not play."

She unlocked the door and we entered the

house. She had very good taste. Her home was neat and clean, just the way I like it. I followed her lead, taking off my shoes at the door, so we wouldn't track the dirty rain on her hardwood floors. We then headed straight for her bedroom. I sat on her fluffy queen-size bed and told her to strip for me. Angel turned on some soft music I've never heard before and did her best to slow hip roll as she removed her clothes. Her body was much better than I expected. I quickly stripped down to my boxers so I could lay back and enjoy the show.

"Is that for me?" She pointed to my erection.

"Only if you want it." I removed my boxers so she could get a better look.

"Can I show you how much I do?"

Before I could answer, she had her soft lips wrapped around my hardness. Her head game was on point. If I let her keep going with it, I was gonna bust in her warm deep throat, and I wasn't ready. I pulled her all the way onto the bed with me and then flipped her onto her stomach and pulled her up on her hands and knees. I ran the tip of my hardness up and down her slit, teasingly, tickling her clit to get her nice and wet before sliding deep inside her from the back, just the way she told me she wanted to be fucked over the phone. I long stroked her nice and hard. I had her moaning loudly and pulling her own hair.

"Yes. Get this pussy, baby. Get it, make it yours," she purred.

Hearing that made me hit it harder, turning her moans into screams of passion. I flipped her on her back so I could get face-to-face with her. She tried to lock her short legs around me so I couldn't continue to punish her wetness, so I pinned her knees and pounded her just like that before slowing down. I released her legs and slowed my hip roll, enjoying wave after wave as she came for me. She felt so good I couldn't hold back any longer. I held out to the last second and then pulled out and released all over her belly. Angel took me in her hand, milking every last drop out of me, but she wasn't done with me yet. She took me in her mouth, sucking my thickness until I was nice and hard again. This bitch is an animal! I was tired, so I pulled her on top of me.

"Show me you want a nigga in your life. Make this dick yours," I encouraged her as she gave me her all. She rode me like a real cowgirl, hard and fast.

When I felt her legs start to tremble, I took over by bouncing with my hands, gripping her hips, until she came hard, soaking me. I rolled her off of me and got back deep in her wetness. I fucked her until I got off for the second time. We took a quick shower together and then she rushed me to work, promising to pick me up afterward so she could feed me a real home-cooked meal. Did I mention she was a vegetarian? One would've never guessed from the way she tried to swallow the dick.

Chapter 5

Family Time

NOW A COUPLE OF MONTHS had pass-

ed, and I had earned my first overnight home pass.

I had used up the hourly passes to go visit my

mother and a few friends. I had also been spending

a lot of time with Angel. Hell, she was the only

person that was trying to see me that wasn't on

bullshit about my situation. So when I was given my

overnight, the first thing I did was call her. I had to

explain the way things had to go on the pass. I let

her know that I had to take it at the address the halfway house had listed as home for me.

"You can make here home for you?"

"And fuck up what we got? I don't think so," I joked and laughed because I didn't think she was being serious. "I gotta take it there because they might drop in on me to see if I'm there, drunk, or getting high."

"Which you don't do none of, sooo?"

"So it won't be an issue for me. Angel, I'ma pretty much use this to really try to reconnect with my kids. Before you go there,

I plan on spreading a few blankets out on the floor and falling asleep with all of my badasses around me. After we pig out on whatever they want. I'm not sure if my wife gonna be there, but I'm not finna lie to you, if she is and wants to talk about us, I'ma do that."

"Babe, I trust you to be the man you are. Just promise me that first thing Monday morning you'll be here sleeping in my bed. I don't want sex, just you holding me while we sleep."

"Ma, why you bullshittin'? You know I can't keep that promise. I'm on brick just thinking about lying next to you." We laughed. "Yeah, you got that," I promised. We changed subjects and talked a little more before I told her that I had to call Donna so she could pick me up. I was surprised by how stand-up Angel was being about it. She didn't show one bit of jealousy or anger. If she was, I couldn't tell.

~ ~ ~

Donna was there on time to pick me up. She was looking good, but she was still not talking about giving me none, so it was the furthest thing from my mind. When we made it to the house, she was right back out the door like a half hour or so later. No, she wasn't running off. I had asked the kids what they wanted to eat and the movies they wanted to watch. So she went to go pick everything up. Donna asked me to ride with her, but I didn't wanna chance it. Ms. Carrol had made it so clear that she didn't wanna lose her money. She informed me that if I wasn't there when the officer stopped by that this would be my first and last weekend pass. She also told me that I could get sent back to prison as well.

After playing hard with the kids and having fun like we did before I went away, I sat down with them and talked about everything that was going on with them as we ate pizza, candy, and hot wings, washing it all down with cold soda. I got a little free time from the kids because they were into some funny movie that their mother had picked out for them. I used this time to help Donna relax more in the bath she had gone to take.

 Okay, I was on some get-back shit for all of them mornings she teased me with thoughts of getting some. I crept in the bathroom and locked the door behind me. She had it all decked out with nice scented candles burning, a classic R&B CD playing some good old Babyface, and a tub full of bubbles. She was chillin' so hard I thought she had fallen asleep. The best part was she didn't know I was in there with her. Well, she pretended not to know. I removed my shirt. I already knew I wasn't getting none, so that's all I took off. Then I kneeled beside the tub and softly kissed her lips. Without a second of hesitation, she returned my kiss. I then mass-aged her neck, shoulders, and chest. I gave her the most sensual massage I knew how to give, until I heard soft moans escaping her lips.

 "Bae, this feels sooo good. Thank you!"

"For what? I ain't finished yet." I took off the rest of my clothes, still not planning on having sex with her. I was just enjoying the moment with her.

"Do you still love me for real? I mean after all that time apart, or you just here to punish me for not being there for you like I should've been?"

"Yes, I'm still in love with you. I told you, I understand what you went through. I feel you should've trusted me more, but let's not ruin this here with talk. Just sit back and enjoy my touch. Let me finish relearning every inch of my beautiful wife's body." I climbed into the tub with her, spilling water on the floor.

"Wait, bae."

"Shhhh. Don't talk. I know what you need right now."

I covered her face with kisses, working my way down her body with my lips and skillful hands. I massaged her feet while staring into her soft brown eyes. I slid my hands slowly up her legs until I could feel the warmth of her wetness. She moaned and opened her legs wider as I dipped my fingers in and out of her. Massaging her button at the same time the way I remembered she liked me to. Within moments, her legs began to tremble, and she dug her fingernails into my strong forearms. I knew I could have her because I had her right where she needed to be, but I wanted her to beg for it like I had been doing since I got home. Donna took hold of my length, gently stroking it as we kissed passionately. I wanted her so fuckin' bad, but I held on by pulling her hand away. I was just about to dip my head under water and have a taste of her when my stepson knocked on the door.

"Daddy, come watch the other movie with us."

"Okay! Here I come." I shook my head at his

timing and stood up to get out of the tub.

"Wait, I want you to cum for me," Donna said, taking hold of my hand to stop me from leaving.

"No you don't." I pulled away and got out of the tub. "I want you to want me when you're ready, not because you're caught up in a moment that I manipulated you into." I cut her words off with a kiss and then dried off, dressed, and rejoined the kids on the floor in front of the TV.

~ ~ ~

Sometime before the last movie ended, me and all the kids fell asleep on the floor. We were all together just how I pictured us being. I'm guessing it was after one in the morning when Donna tiptoed into the front room and woke me up.

"Bae, come get in the bed with me. I wanna sleep in my husband's arms too." She pretended to pout, crossing her arms the way the kids did when they wanted something.

I got up and followed, her dressed in a little blue lace teddy that stopped midway on her apple bottom. I could see she wasn't wearing panties. I was instantly erect and aroused. I closed the door behind us, and she helped me undress as we kissed. Breaking our kiss, Donna pushed me down on the bed to pull off my boxers.

"I need my husband," she told me before dropping down and taking my hardness in her mouth.

I was loving the way she had me feeling. It was so different than it was with Angel, I guess because there were real feelings here, and with her it was just lust. I pulled Donna onto the bed with me until she was sitting on my face. She allowed herself to enjoy my tongue work for awhile before she turned around and put us in the 69 position, where we stayed until she couldn't take it anymore and let her nectar rain down on me. That shit turned me on even more. My joint was so hard it hurt. I spun her around, flipping her under me and drove deep inside of her warmth. I gave her my trusted long stroke. She was lovin' every inch of it, moaning my name and clawing my shoulders. I guess she remembered the tattoo on my back and didn't want to damage it. We tore into one another until the morning sun kissed the sky, and then fell asleep. The next thing I knew I was being served breakfast in bed.

When I got up the kids were all gone. The boys were at football practice and the girls were both gone by their aunt's house to get their hair done. With the house to ourselves, Donna and I used the time to really talk. She went first.

"I know you just got out, and I didn't want to stress you with all my shit. My back is better now, and I'm looking for a job."

"Donna, we're a family. It don't matter if I'm still in prison. You should've told me what was going on. It's always something I can do."

"See, you mad. That's why I didn't wanna tell you."

"I'm not mad. This is my thinking face." I smiled. "The halfway house takes 35 percent of my money before taxes just for being there. I do have a little saved I can give you to give the landlord to get him off our back. He should be okay if we pay off two of the three months that you're behind, and I want you to set up a budget with the utilities."

"Okay. They said if I can get caught up they'll put me on a budget."

"Put us on a budget," I corrected her. "We're in this together for better or for worse."

"I don't want you to get in trouble and get sent

back to prison for this."

"Well, let's pray I don't get caught. Because if I do, that's where I'm going."

After our heartfelt talk, it was pretty much time for me to get back to the halfway house. When we got there, I had her wait and ran in to grab the cash I had stashed in my room. I took all of it except for $300 because I had to hold on to something for myself—my "just in case" funds. I put over $1,500 in her hands to take care of the house with.

Shae was standing there waiting for me to say my goodbyes to my wife so she could talk to me.

"Who's she? The bitch you've been giving my dick to?"

"Nope, wrong bitch. Try again," I joked. She hit me. "Donna, stop it! She just cool. We ain't ever done nothing, and ain't thinking about it."

"How do I know that?" Donna asked, letting her

jealousy show.

"Because I just told you so, and you should trust me to do better."

"I do trust you. I don't trust that bitch. I know when a bitch want mine."

"Look, I gotta go, so stop all that. I ain't fucking her, okay?"

"Okay, I hear you. Now give me a kiss." I did. "Til death do us part, nigga, you're mine." She smiled and then pulled off leaving me standing there shaking my head.

I walked back in the building. Just like we did always, I grabbed a couple of Brisks and kicked it with Shae out in the courtyard. I paid her to wash and press the few outfits I owned. My mind was on how I needed to make something shake for my family. A nigga wasn't feeling this broke shit at all, but I promised myself that I was gonna do my best not to pick up that pack and get back to hustling when I got out. On the inside of them prison walls niggas don't know how hard it is out here in the real world trying to live the legal way of life. I thought about what Money Bones told me about him getting back in the game. But he was only fooling around selling weed until he got his business up and running good. It sounds good, but he had almost a hundred G's to start with, and I'd have to start from the bottom. So I'ma leave that alone, plus a nigga way too grown to be working for a nigga. I could get through this little bill situation Donna had us in, and I could do it without hustling nothing illegal. I just needed to think, so I did what I always did when I needed to sort things out in my head. I picked up my pen and notebook and went to work on finishing my story that I had now titled, The Hard Way Out. By the time dinner was done, I had a plan.

Chapter 6

The Plan

MONDAY MORNING I WAS on business.

Angel dropped me off at work after I made good on my promise to lie with her for the couple hours I had before work. Yeah, you know that wasn't all we did. I fucked her so good that morning she gave me $400. When I asked what the money was for, she told me that she just wanna help me in any way she could. I was wowed because I hadn't told her about the money issues or anything pertaining to Donna.

But then I remembered that I had bitched to her about the halfway house taking all my money in the past, so maybe that's what brought it on. Nooo, it was my down stroke.

At work, I found the break room empty as I passed by it on my way to the boss's office. I walked in on him getting some head from a dusty-looking hype bitch. I remember seeing the crack whore walking the National Street strip a few times when I stopped on Sixteenth Street to cash my check and get the money orders from the halfway house.

"Say, Jim! Holla at me when you done."

"Oh shit!" He jumped to his feet knocking the whore to the floor. "This isn't what it . . ."

I cut him off. "Look, don't trip, it's all good. Just holla at me when you done, and lock this door next time."

WIFE

Jim didn't say anything to me until our first break. I don't believe it was because he was avoiding me. It was more because we were really busy that day since one of the drunk Latinos didn't show up for work, and I couldn't understand the other two without him there to interpret for me.

"What's up? What is it you needed to see me about so badly?"

"I need you to cut me two checks for a minute." I saw his eyes widen. I guess he thought I was about to try to blackmail him or put my press game on him for what I witnessed that morning. Well, yeah, I was gonna use it to my advantage knowing he didn't want something like that getting out. But, no, I wasn't finna blackmail him. Jim was alright with me. He knew my predicament with the halfway house, so he would let me off work early sometimes and still pay me for the full day, even when I came in for overtime on the weekends. Jim would pay me for the whole eight hours when we would only work like three or four. "Jim, don't go there. We're cool on that shit with that bitch."

"That's good to know. So what is it?" Relief replaced the worry that was on his face.

"Well, I got some money issues at home that I need to handle. But I can't with giving them people my checks."

"I think I know what you need from me, but tell me just to be sure we're on the same page," he said as he leaned against a stack of old wooden boxes.

"I need you to put my overtime on a check on its own, but you can't adjust the hours on my other check because all they look at really is the hours when it's handed in," I explained.

"Sure, I can work that out for you. Is that all you need from me?"

"No. I'ma need you to pick a better-looking bitch than that hoe you had." We laughed, and I returned to the floor to get my job done.

With that outta the way, my day was going pretty good. That's up until one of the drunk Latinos knocked over a ladder that sent one of the other workers crashing down like fifteen feet into a deep, dirty pit of water. We were emptying the twenty-foot pit, bucket by bucket, because the sump pump had gone out on us. The man that was knocked in the water couldn't swim and was panicking, pulling at the rope we were using to haul out the five-gallon buckets of water and sour grain.

I rushed and grabbed the line, holding on to it with all I had in me while trying to keep my footing on the muddy, slippery, wet floor.

"Hey, muthafucka, don't just stand there! Help!"

The Mexican started talking shit in Spanish but

never made a move to help me. The rope was digging into my hands and my feet were sliding, so I yelled for help as loudly as I could. My cousin Rome came running. I was so happy I had talked him into getting a job there with me.

"What's wrong?" he asked right away, taking hold of the rope.

"Help me pull Rick up outta that shit. That dumb muthafucka pushed the ladder down in the pit with him on it. You know them walls too slippery for him to climb out."

Rome helped me pull Rick up, but he was too far out to reach the landing on his own. "I got this. Go help him." It was time to put all that working out I'd been doing to use.

Once Rome got Rick safely on solid ground, he was mad as hell. The man looked like something from a low-budget horror flick. Rick was hot, cussing the Mexican out in between gagging and throwing up the water that had gotten in his mouth and nose. After the near-death incident, Jim gave us all the rest of the day off and fired the Latino for it and being drunk on the job.

We showered and got changed out of our work clothes. Then as me and Rome were walking out to his gold 2000 Pontiac Bonneville, the Mexican and his buddies ran up on us talking shit in Spanish. Now I don't speak Spanish, but I'm from the streets and understand war in every language. So I was ready for the wild swing drunky took at my head. I easily sidestepped the slow haymaker and caught him with a vicious combination of my own. The hard right cross followed by a left uppercut to the chin put him right on his ass.

His good ol' buddy wasn't on the same page because he just kinda stood there in shock as me and my cousin tap-danced on his friend's head. We didn't want him to feel left out, so we beat his ass for not helping his guy. He should've known rule #5 of the streets: If you come together, you fight together, or you run together, but you never leave your homie to fend for himself when it's two on one. After that, Rome dropped me off at Angel's. Something told me that I should keep her around and happy. Hell, if shit didn't work out the way I planned and I got sent back, I was gonna need someone to be in my corner. It's not like I didn't know how Donna would do me. I'm just saying, she took off on me before.

Chapter 7

Donna

"BITCH, GUESS WHO I seen at Playmakers today?"

"I don't wanna guess, so just spit it out. It's probably one of the many dicks you've sucked," I shot at my best friend, Mary. She almost always had something to tell me about somebody. I didn't have time for her guessing games right now. I was going crazy trying to make room in this little-ass bedroom for Ray to come home from that dumbass place he was in today.

"Nope, it's not one of mines this time." She laugh-ed. "This dick all yours, hoe."

That caught my attention. I knew she better not tell me she saw Ray with that punk-ass blue jean bitch he'd been spending time with at the halfway house, or I was gonna give him a good welcome-home ass kicking instead of that pot roast and stuff I'd been slaving over for him. "Mary, just tell me who it is already? Damn!"

"Vince."

"You lying?" I hoped she was lying because I didn't need that shit in my life right now with Ray back. I know he said he understood why I dealt with another nigga while he was locked up, but that's easy to do when he didn't have to deal with the dude.

"No, for real. It was him and June. He told me to

have you call him. Talking about he miss you and all that. I told him I wouldn't make any promises. But he still gave me his number to put in my phone, just in case you wanted it. With his fine ass. Donna, I know your hubby back in your life now an' shit, but he ain't doing shit with his life right now. Not like Vince."

"Mary, don't go there about my husband. He just got out, and he ain't trying to go back no time soon. My baby working a nine-to-five. Hell, I still can't believe he gotta real job or even that he puts his checks in my hand every week with no questions asked. You need to get somebody in your life like I got."

"Bitch, when is you happy with something like that? Fuck that simple life shit. I need a nigga that's ballin' hard and likes to spend it on me at the snap of my fingers. If I remember right, you the one who put me up on game. Now you trying to switch up on me."

"I told you that I was just fucking around until Ray got home and seen what he was on with me. You know how fucked up shit got for me for a minute. Any other nigga would've booked on a bitch that was doing worse than him, but he didn't. Ray still here and wanna be here. I am gonna make my marriage work."

"I hear you, but, bitch, I ain't telling you to leave your man. I'm just saying call Vince and see what he talking like. It ain't like his ass didn't know you were married when y'all was fucking around before he went to jail. Maybe he'll be cool with being your side piece." She giggled like a foolish schoolgirl.

"I don't know, but give me the number. I do need to see what he on. I don't wanna be the reason Ray catches another case."

WIFE

She gave me the number, and I stored it in my phone under my aunt Kat just in case Ray ever went through my phone. He wouldn't be suspicious of it knowing how much I love my auntie. Damn, I couldn't believe he was really coming home. Looking at Vince's number, I decided to call after I got off the phone with Mary.

"What up, who this?" he answered.

"Who do you want it to be? I mean, you're the one who asked me to call you."

"Oh snap! Dee, I just don't answer unknown numbers. You know that."

"Vince, what do you want? I can tell you now that ain't nothing changed with us. You made your choice when you made me leave off that visit instead of that dumbass bitch that put your silly ass in there," I told him, checking on the food I was cooking.

"Dee, don't be like that. I told you what was up with that. Say, I'm finna come over there so we can talk, and don't try an' tell me you're not there. I just seen the car when I passed through them ways a minute ago."

"Vince, please don't come over here. It's not a good time."

"What? You got some nigga there?"

I could hear the anger in his voice. "No, not some nigga. My husband's out and he's on his way here now." I hated to tell him that, but he knew the deal when we started messing around.

"Yeah, well I hope the nigga can buy you a new car because I'm coming to get my shit, bitch!"

"Wow. I got your bitch, nigga! I'm trying to be nice. I didn't say we couldn't talk, just not right now." I heard the front door open and close and knew it was my husband because I had given him a key the

76

day I had the locks changed. "Let me call you tomorrow, okay?"

"How come you can't get away and meet me now? I gotta taste for some of that sweet pussy. Tell me, Dee, can that nigga eat that pussy like I can?"

"Boy, stop. Bye!" I laughed. "I'll see if I can, but if not I'll see you tomorrow." He agreed, and we ended the call just as Ray's arms wrapped around my waist from behind.

"Honey, I'm home!" he sang jokingly. Then he kissed my neck.

I turned around in his arms and kissed his lips. "It feels good to hear you say that." I kissed him again. "No more dealing with them people and their bullshit at that place."

"You can say that again." He pulled away from me. "Where's the kids?" he asked, walking into the kitchen to put his nose in my pots.

"I sent them to Tarn's house for the night so I can have you all to myself."

"That's just selfish. Unless you're planning on getting nice and loud for me?" He stuck his hand down my pants and pulled me to him. His sexy black self knew just how to turn me on.

"I'ma do whatever you like," I told him, sucking on his tongue when he kissed me. "But first go put your things up. I made room for you in the drawers and closet. This food should be done by the time you finish with that." I pulled the cornbread out of the hot oven.

"That's right. Feed, fuck, and suck me. And I ain't tripping if it ain't in that order either," he said, laughing on his way to the bedroom.

"As long as you return the pleasure."

We ate and then Ray wanted to go out for a walk

down by the lakefront after he dropped some money off to the kids and paid my sister to keep them there another day. When we made it to the lakefront, it was too cold for me to be out there walking. Hell, it was December, and snowing out.

On the way down there, I was glad he didn't ask to drive, but I wondered why. Maybe because the car was a step down from what he was used to. Whatever the reason, I was glad he didn't because I didn't need Vince's petty ass to see him, or his fool ass just might take the car back for real. It wasn't like it was a Benz or a Lexus, it was just an old 1985 Ford, but it was also all I had to get me and the kids around until we could save up to get something else. "Yeah, I think I'ma go see Vince ass tomor-row, and if I have to put this pussy on him, then I'ma do what I gotta do to help him get his.

Chapter 8

Donna

SO I GOT INTO it with Ray's baby mama, Rhonnie, over the phone today. I couldn't believe the bitch had the balls to tell me that I would always be second to her and that my husband would always come running when she called. That bitch made me so fuckin' mad I tried to fight Ray.

"Donna, you're trippin' on me because my daughter wants me to bring her sisters over and have a sleepover. Do you see how stupid that is?"

"Don't call me fuckin' stupid!" I rushed him only because I knew he wouldn't hit me. "You're taking up for the bitch? You taking her side over mine?"

"I'm not taking nothing. I'm just saying that it's kids that—"

I slapped the words right outta his mouth. He allowed me to hit him a few more times before he grabbed me and put me on my ass. No, he didn't hit me back. He grabbed my hands, spun me around, and kicked my feet out from under me and placed me on the ground. The look he had in his eyes frightened the hell outta me, but watching him walk out the door was what hurt the most. And truth be told, I wasn't even mad about the shit we got into it about. I was mad at Vince. Just like the bitch he was, the nigga took the car back a few days after I went to see him—after I put it on him real good the way I knew he liked it. But that wasn't enough for him. Vince got mad because I wasn't trying to hear that shit he was talking about me leaving my husband for him. So sometime in the middle of the night, his punk ass came and took the car.

Anyway, that's the real reason I was mad. Ray wasn't gone long, and when he walked in, I made it my business to make up with my boo. I knew he didn't buy the story I fed him about the car being towed for unpaid parking tickets and that I didn't have the title because it was in the glove box. But Ray didn't press the issue. He went to work trying to find a way to get us another one.

It was just five days before Christmas, and I didn't have all of my shopping done. Ray had gotten laid off from his job, so money was back tight again. Yeah, he found another job through a temp agency right away. He had the same pay, but different hours. He now worked second shift and a whole lot of overtime. So until we found a car we could afford, my mom let us use her car since she worked until closing as a barmaid.

All I had to do was drop her off at work after I took Ray to the spot where the agency's van was to pick him up and take him to and from the job site. He had it set up that way just in case he had to take the city bus to get there one day. I could see all of it was hard on him and he was really trying to stay on a straight line. I was proud that he was holding on, but I couldn't keep living with my head barely above water like some punk bitch. That's why I was here with Vince's face planted between my legs. Hey, I had five kids with needs, as well as my own. So if feeding this trick-ass nigga a little bit of this good-good was going to help me get some of that done, so be it.

Vince knew just what I needed. He hit me with a

couple of rollers and some Smirnoff, and I was gone. I loved my husband to death, but we weren't on the same page the way we were before he went away. Ray didn't get high, and he never drank. I'd never seen him drunk. Vince got me used to partying like that when I was with him. I knew I was being a hypocrite doing what I was doing. But this was the last time I was going to fool with those pills and anything else that had to do with Vince.

Even though I fucked Vince in every position he could think of and fed him as much of my cookie he could stand, I didn't suck his dick. Yeah, all of it was wrong, but to go home and kiss my husband when the next man's dick had been in my mouth would be too wrong. Especially when he just came home from working his butt off trying to keep a roof over our heads.

At some point, I fell asleep in Vince's arms. It was

the constant ringing of my phone that woke me up. I quickly snatched it up and saw it was Ray calling for me to pick him up. I checked the time and found out that I was almost an hour late. I rushed to get dressed so I could get home, knowing he was on his way there. When I left Vince, I was two G's richer, thanks to the trick-a-dick-ass nigga.

The streets were bad, and the snow was really coming down. I made a plan to use it to my advantage. My husband knew I didn't like to drive in bad weather like this, so I'd be good on that, but I didn't know how I was gonna explain not answering the phone. I'd just cross that road when it came up. I knew Ray was mad as hell that he had to catch the city bus, but he'd get over it.

When I made it home, he wasn't there yet. I took a shower and did some crying. It's real fucked up when you hurt your own feelings. Afterward, I got in bed and just lay there. I picked up the phone and saw that it was now almost two in the morning and he wasn't home yet. On top of that he stopped blowing my phone up. I was worried now. I called and called his phone, but it kept going to voicemail. Now tears were really coming down. I got outta bed and went to the couch and sat looking out the front window. Finally my phone rang.

"Hello? Bae, are you alright?" I answered, truly concerned.

"How come you ain't been answering the fuckin' phone?" he snapped at me. "I had to walk to my mother's house in all this fuckin' snow because I missed the last bus waiting on you. I couldn't call nobody to pick me up because my damn phone died from callin' your ass."

"I'm sorry. Bae, I fell asleep. You know I went to the doctor today, and these pills he put me on knocked me out," I lied. "I didn't even pick Mama up from work."

"I know. She called me worried too." His tone softened.

"When you coming home?"

"In the morning, if you're not coming to pick me up."

"Bae, I'm looking out the window and the car is plowed in. Can your mother bring you?"

"It's late and she asleep. Anyway, her car's snowed in too." I heard him exhale. "Bae, I'm still cold as hell, my feet froze, I'm tired as hell, and it's late. I'll be there in the morning."

I knew I was wrong for what I was about to do, but for some reason I didn't believe he was at his mother's house. It was a long-ass walk from the south side to the north side in the snow. I knew that bitch Rhonnie's house was much closer. "Ray, if you don't come to this house tonight, then don't come back to it. I know you don't expect me to believe you walked all the way over to your mother's in the snow. Fuck you and that bitch you're with!" I hung up in his face but answered the phone when he called right back. "What!"

"Why you hang up on me like that? I'm at my mother's. On everything I love, I am. And ain't no bitch here with me."

"I don't want to get back in the habit of you not coming home. I don't know . . . I wanna believe you, but . . ."

"Okay, fuck it. I'm on my way. I love you."

"I love you too."

He made it there in less than an hour. I knew right then that the shit with me partying with Vince was over.

Chapter 9

I'm Getting Tired

"MAN, BRO, THIS SHIT'S fucked up. I put in all that work just to be laid off." I vented my frustrations about working for a temp agency. "The only good thing is that it's not gonna be until after New Year's."

"Bruh, you know if you need anything I got you," my homie T-Bay let me know as he drove me home after my visit with my parole officer. Yeah, I had three years of that to do after the halfway house.

"I know, bro. That was good looking with that Suburban. It's just what we needed." I bought the truck with my check the night after the night I had to walk from the south side in a blizzard. I think an old head from the hood told me a story just like that when I was a kid.

"I told you she was a runner." He made a left, heading east on Center Street. "I can't believe he gave it to you for $900."

"Yeah, that old man cool for that there. He said he knows how it is to have a big family and not be able to get around like you need to, and he wanted it to go to a family that really needed it."

"What you got planned for it? I know you finna do something nice."

"Hell, I'ma put some sounds in it and that's pretty much it. I ain't got it like that no more, remember? Plus Donna be in it more than me anyway. We really need two cars for real."

"Bruh, you can use the Caddy for as long as you need to. It's just sitting there behind the crib anyway. I rather my brotha have it than one of my wife's lazy-ass brothers get it and fuck it up." T-Bay took me back to his house to give me the keys to his white 1997 Cadillac and some cash.

"What's this for?"

"Bruh, it's for whatever you wanna do with it. Since you ain't ready to get your hustle on yet. Don't trip, I'm not doing shit you wouldn't do for me."

"Good lookin'. You and Moe can't keep doing this. I know it's love, but I'm trying to see if I can't make it the square way."

"Bruh, I told Carlos about you, and he really wants to meet you."

"It's tempting, but I'm good. I didn't know he dealt with anything besides weed, or did you tell him what I used to do?"

"Yeah, I told him. That's why he wants to fuck with you. His people talkin' about flooding him with it all, and he need somebody who can move it."

"Why don't you just push both?"

"I thought about it. Even talked it over with my wife. She thinks it's too risky, talking about niggas gon rob and kill us for that shit."

"What? A muthafucka will run up on the weed man faster than a nigga with work. Especially a nigga pushing bricks. It's more likely for him to have an army behind him than it is for the weed man. She trippin'."

"Maybe if you tell her that shit she'll fall in line with it. I know she would if you get down with me."

"That's not finna happen, but you can count on me for whatever else. Hell, we can just make her think it's me when it's all you if you wanna do it so bad."

We carried on our conversation as we went down to his game room that was located in the basement. There he pulled out a sixty-five-pound bundle of kush and sat it on the pool table.

"Bruh, help me get this together so I won't be in this bitch all day?"

"Do you got a extra scale?" I asked, and he set everything up we needed to break down and package up the weed. I can't lie, the allure of fast money had me really thinking that getting back in the game wouldn't be such a bad thing, with my job ending in a few weeks and not know how long it would be before they found me something else. And to keep it real with you, I was kinda sick of my guys giving me handouts like I was a kid. "You know what, Tee? Let me hold a couple of these zips, and tell your guy I'll meet up with him." T-Bay stared like a crackhead that had just found a sack of the hard, white work. "You set it up, and let me know when and where. Hell, it won't hurt to see what he talking. But this for you, not me." I made my actions clear to him. But I wasn't clear with myself really.

~ ~ ~

When I made it home, Donna and the kids were gone. So I gathered my things for work and hit the streets with the $500 bro gave me. Normally, I would've put most of it in my wife's hands to take care of those household needs or whatever her and the kids needed, but not today. I was on my way to do something for me. Yeah, a nigga was sick of dressing in Wal-Mart's finest. I stopped at an urban clothing store called Number One Sports and bought two outfits. One was for the weekend to wear when I took the wife out for dinner and drinks.

And the other was to bring the New Year in. The outfit was something I started doing when I was a wild teen. Peachee, my first wife, had told me that who I brought in the New Year with was who I would spend the year with. I just took it a step farther and made sure I always had money in my pocket and was dressed in something new, so I'd have money and nice things the rest of the year. Hey, I was a kid, but it worked for me.

After shopping, I headed straight to work. The whole time I was there slaving my butt off, lifting hot, heavy steel plates from one place to another. My mind was on the two ounces of weed I had gotten from T-Bay. I didn't really want to get out there, but it was only until I found another job once this one ended. When it was break time, I called Angel and vented to her how hard things were getting for me working for the temp agency. I also hinted around about the idea of selling weed to keep a little something in my pockets until they assigned me another job or I found one.

"Assa, you shouldn't go from one extreme to another. Remember, you're not trying to go back. Let me help you. I might can't give the type of money you're used to, but what I have is yours if it'll help."

"Thanks for the offer! But that's part of my issue, I'm sick of the handouts. I'm used to getting my own. If I do decide to do it, I got a lot of family and friends that smoke, so I can fool with them and be okay. As long as I stay focused on finding a job fast, I'll be good."

"Well, I'm here if you need me." She paused. "So am I going to see you later?"

I hadn't really been spending much time with her because of all of the overtime and being at home with Donna. "I gotta work late and I won't be off until morning." T-Bay was calling. "I'll call you later. I gotta take this call from my brotha." I ended the call with her, promising her again that I would call on my next break. Bro was calling to tell me that Carlos wanted us to get together after the New Year because he wasn't going to be in town until then. That was cool with me because it gave me more time to think of how I was going to do everything. I'd be kinda middle-manning things, which wouldn't be so bad I guessed. But Angel was right, I didn't need to go from one extreme to another. Selling dime bags to my family wasn't an extreme to me. I believed it could work since now Donna was about to be working with my cousin at FedEx and another shipping company. I wouldn't have to stress as much on the household stuff, but I still had to get a job quick, or something, to keep my PO happy and off my back. It was bad enough he was making me

go see a psychologist for my depression issues.

Chapter 10

A Few More Cracks

March 2008

AS YOU CAN SEE, I made it through the New Year's Day celebrations in one piece. It's rough in the Mil on the first of the year with all the partying and guns blasting to close out the past year. One can easily get hit by a stray bullet that was shot in the air for fun, or that was meant for somebody else. I brought the year in working right in the middle of the chaos with my wife at the nightclub her mother works in. We had a real good time, and I was doing pretty okay saving a little money from my little side sales.

The job ended just like I knew it would, but I was good. I did what I had to do to get by while running from job interview to job interview. I even applied at other temps.

Donna and I shared a nice romantic Valentine's Day. I took her out to a nice Oriental bistro, where her ass fell in love with their plum wine. Since the day was all about her, I paid the $25 for the bottle to-go for her. It was a good thing I had the cash from the weed to spend to make her happy. All I could think of was all of the days like this I missed with her. Anyway, we capped off the night locked in one another's arms at home.

Now just a month later I was getting this shit . . .

"Nigga, do you really expect me to believe that

you get up and leave this house every gotdamn morning and come home at night with nothing?" Donna snapped. "Okay, I'll play boo da fool with you on that shit. But I know you, and I know you're not just helping Moe and them line their pockets and not your own! It ain't that much brotherly love in the world when you're broke!"

"Wow! Tell me how you really feel then, Donna." I stood up from sitting on the bed. "I don't gotta lie to you. I'm doing all I can to find a job. I even signed up for that work-a-day-pay-a-day bullshit at the temp until somethin' come up for me. I sit in the muthafucka all fuckin' day, waiting. I told you they pick all of their friends first, then whatever Mexicans in there, before me." I stepped closer to her. "And I told you, I'm not fooling with bro 'n'em like that. It's not what I wanna do anymore. I've lived that life they're living and lost everything over and over. I'm trying something new. But if that's not what you want, you need to find a nigga that's on that. Just know that I ain't gonna be down forever!"

"I can't tell, nigga! I didn't marry a scary-ass nigga. I don't know what happened to you in prison, but you need to get it together! I'm not gonna be taking care of no grown-ass man when I got five kids to slave for!" she told me, fighting back tears.

"So what? You want me to leave?"

I'm not finna sit here and lie to you; it hurt when she said, "Yeah." But I didn't let her see that it did. I didn't say anything else to her while I gathered my stuff and walked out. In the car, I called my sister and asked her if I could stay with her for a while since she had a spare bedroom.

"Of course you can. What happened with you and Donna?"

"Some bullshit. I'll tell you about it when I get

there. I'm finna be on my way now." I looked back up at the house and saw Donna watching me from the window. I just shook my head and pulled off. Fuck it, if this was what she wanted, she got it.

"Alright, if I'm not here, just wait. I'm going to run and get an extra key from the office."

Sheeka lived in low-income housing, or the Hillside Projects. The building she was in consisted of four units, and all four apartments were occupied by single mothers. I spotted my sister and the twins walking up just as I turned into the parking lot. I got out and followed them into the apartment. As soon as we got settled I told her how things went down and explained that I needed to come to her house so my PO could come by and do a home visit without me having to explain anything other than me and my wife was taking a break or whatever it was.

"Big brother, don't worry about it. Donna just frustrated right now." She took a deep pull off of her blunt. In a few days she'll be begging you to come back home after she calms down. Mark my words."

"Sheeka, that girl is stubborn as hell, but I hope you're right, because this is dumb as hell." I stood up from the kitchen table where we sat talking away from the kids while she smoked. "I'ma go lay down for a minute. My head hurts, and them people at the temp place worked the hell outta me today. They had me moving the stuff in their office around so they could wax the floors or something. I don't know. I just did it because I needed a little money and to show them that I'll work just as hard as the Mexicans."

"I hear you. I'ma take the girls out so you can get some rest."

"You don't gotta do that, I'm good. But if you just

wanna go somewhere, you can use the car." I gave her the keys and went into the bedroom and lay down on the unmade bed.

Alone in the dark, I wondered if I was the one wrong for not doing more? Fuck no! I really just took care of her grown ass before she got a job. Hell, it was because of me she even got the damn job. Donna acted like I was taking money from them or something now that I wasn't working steady hours. I was making like $100 or more a day off the little weed I had. I could have been making way more, but I was not out there like that, and I had to miss money when I was sitting in that temp, praying to get picked for work. Fuck her! I picked up my cell and called Angel, who I hadn't seen in awhile. I fed her a few half truths that she ate up. Not because I had to, but because it wasn't her business what went on with me and my wife.

"I don't think you should be alone right now," she said. "I was on my way out, but you should let me come pick you up."

I agreed, hung up with her, and then called my sister and told her that she could keep the car and where I was going.

"Brother, could you leave me a blunt? I'll pay you for it when my baby daddy bring me this money he owes me."

"It's good, Sheeka. Keep your money. I'll leave it in your room on the dresser."

"Alright, thanks!"

I got on up, jumped in the shower, and changed clothes for my little rendezvous with Angel. While I waited for her to get there, I called an old friend of mine that wasn't in the street life so much. He was more guilty by association. Baabie was a club owner and knew a lot of people around the city that owned businesses, so I reached out to him for help finding work.

"Assa, that's nothing. I'll talk to a few of my guys, and if you want, you can pick up a few days down here at the club as a bouncer. It don't pay much, but it's something to keep them people off your back until you can do better."

He was right, my PO was bound to start tripping about me not working for so long. "I can do that, thanks! I'll come in tomorrow night and see what I gotta do to get things together for you in that bitch."

"Sounds like a plan. I'll see you then."

We ended the call just as Angel was calling to let me know she was in the parking lot. She told me to hurry because she didn't like the way the thugs out there were looking at her. I told her that they just trying to see if she's the police, but stayed on the line with her until I was ready to walk out the door.

I briskly went down the stairs, almost running into the woman that lived in the unit right below my sister's. She smiled as we made eye contact.

"My bad, I didn't hurt you, did I?"

"No, I'm alright."

"Okay. Maybe next time I see you I won't be in such a hurry." I smiled back as I continued toward the exit.

"Hey, you must be with that quiet light-skinned girl in C."

"Yeah, she my sister. Why?" I knew she was just being nosey, but she was pretty and had the body of a stripper. I made a mental note to ask my sister about her when I got back.

"Oh, no reason. She just don't talk to nobody and I'm curious," she admitted.

I headed on out the door. The first thing I did when I got in the car with Angel was give her a hug and kiss on the neck. She pretended like it sent a shiver down her body.

"I've missed you," she told me, pulling out of the lot.

"If you did, why haven't I heard from you lately?"

"To be honest, I wanted to see if you would call me, and I'm trying to show you that I don't mind sharing you with your wife. But just her."

"Well, I don't know how things gonna go with that there, but I don't want to talk about her all night. Let's just chill the way we do, okay?"

"Is that what you need?"

"Yep, and to be held tight as I'm deep, deep off in you."

For the rest of the ride we didn't talk because she had gotten a call. We just held hands as she drove. Now here was a woman that didn't mind me not having all of the cars and bling as long as I was trying to do better for myself. But still I couldn't see myself with her for the rest of my life. Yeah, some may call me a pussy-whipped muthafucka, but I was far from it. Donna and the kids made me want more outta life. You know, the dream: ranch-style home, kids, dog, cat, and wife. But my whole heart wasn't with her.

"Assa, do you feel up to going out with me to-night?" Angel asked, stopping for a red light.

"I don't care, as long as I don't gotta go home to change." I was dressed in a gray-and-black striped Polo shirt, powder-gray loose fit Levi's, and black Air Force Ones.

"Is it a dress code?" she asked whoever she was talking to on the phone.

Once she ended the call she explained to me that we were invited to a friend of hers birthday bash. I told her I was okay with it. A short time later we were pulling up to a small elegant-looking night-club. I saw guys dressed in sports jackets and ties, women in dresses. The only reason I didn't feel out of place was because

I saw cars in the parking lot sitting on big rims and candy painted. This told me that there were a few hood niggas in there.

When we were seated across from the birthday girl herself, Angel gave me the heads-up that her friends weren't used to seeing her with someone as dressed down as I was and that they may ask me to take the stage because she may or may not have told them about a poem I wrote her. I spent the next hour answering questions while trying to think of something to say if I was called on. Soon the shows started and we sat back and enjoyed all of the men and women who took the stage. They mostly did spoken-word poems, but a few were freestyle raps all done with a live band.

Looking around I saw that all the tables had numbered cards on them. I found out why when the emcee called our number and Angel got up on the stage. She said a few words to the birthday girl and then began to sing a song she had written.

"You were really good. I didn't know you could blow like that," I complimented her when she returned to her seat.

"Thank you! This is a side of me that I don't share to often anymore."

"Why not, when you're so good at it?" I asked, taking a sip of my mixed drink. It was just cranberry juice and soda.

"I don't know. I guess life just gets in the way more than I would like it to," she answered, taking a sip of her wine. "The good thing is I just saved you from being called up there." She smiled.

"Good, because I can't think of nothing to say. And the closest I done came to doing something in front of a crowd like this was a rap battle in prison." We laughed, but I was serious.

As the night went on, we talked and enjoyed the party. Shortly after the cake was cut we called it a night and went back to her place. Once there I gave her what she'd really been missing from me in a few new positions until we fell asleep in the soft light of the early morning.

Chapter 11

The Chief of Security

IT HAD BEEN OVER a month since I had started working at the door of Baabie's club. Donna was still standing her ground about us being broken up, even though we talked on the phone almost daily because of the kids having questions for me.

"Ray, all you're doing is disrespecting yourself working a damn door at that little-ass club."

"Yeah, to you I might be, but I'm doing what I gotta do to be here and keep my promise to my kids.

So if you don't got nothing else to tell me, then I need to get ready to open up."

"What happened to you?" Donna asked, and then hung up.

I didn't see my working at the club as me disrespecting myself. I saw it as an opening to a dream of starting my own business. Working there allowed me to network with more people who owned businesses, as well as those in the streets who all also like to smoke weed.

Many of them liked to smoke but didn't like to deal with the dumb rude corner boys that sold it. So in no time I went from making gas money to putting my brother and his two friends on to help me move the pounds I was now buying. Now before you say you knew I would do this, let me explain. As you know, I was helping T-Bay with Carlos by middle manning everything. Well, I had run into a nigga I knew from my past who said he wanted two pounds of loud and a quarter kilo. But when I brought it to him, his fool ass only bought the dope, talking about he had gotten a better deal on the weed. I was pissed the fuck off, but I still took his money for the dope. The weed, I just broke it down and got it off myself because it's childish to bring work back. "Get in, get gone," has always been my motto.

So I still only sold bags, maybe an ounce or two, but that's it, no matter how much my brothas tried to talk me into getting back down for real. I was also still spending my mornings trying to get work out of the temp agencies. I ran around town from office to office only to be told I wouldn't be getting the job I had applied for. They all gave me messed-up reasons for not hiring me. But the truth behind them all was that I was a felon.

Anyway, I was enjoying myself being a bouncer

at Club Embassy. Most of the crowd that frequent-
ed the spot lived in the area and was pretty cool
with having me there. But there were a few that
didn't take kindly to an outsider telling them they
couldn't enter without ID, nor could they pay me to
look the other way so they could bring guns in.
Now, I'm not strapped, so it would be just dumb of
me to let somebody that I might just have to put out
of the place in with a gun. My only real beef I had
was with this big, almost three hundred-pound,
brown-skin nigga and his clique. His name was Big
J, and I guess he was used to the guy that worked
the door before me being afraid of him. I'm not the
baddest nigga alive, but I haven't met the man that
could put fear in my heart just by being born. I don't
fear the unknown, I respect it. It's in my bloodline
that way. If you're a bully, I'm the bully's bully. I
don't know no other way to be.

So one night I was working the door when this young guy came in with this fine-ass dark-skin woman. I didn't check her out too close because I didn't want to be disrespectful to ol' boy. But she was hard not look at. Baabie and all of his Nigerian friends were eyeing her. The youngsta she was with told me that she was his mother. I couldn't believe it because he had to be around twenty-three or twenty-four years old, and she didn't look much older. Now my mother is only like three years older than me, but you can tell . . . Well, I guess I can tell, because she does tell people that I'm her brother from time to time when we're out. Fuck it, I sent her a drink and she accepted it mouthing thank you to me showing her pretty smile.

Baabie and his buddies took the smile to me as a greenlight for them to try their luck with her. She turned them down. I didn't even try when I saw that.

Hell, I was the one working for these niggas she was turning down. I didn't have anywhere near the money as the rest of the guys trying to get at her. Y'all already know I'm barely making it. Hell, my own wife stopped fucking with me because I was on team Low Cash. My mind wasn't on females anymore. It was all about a come-up, a legal one. Like the old-school rap star once said, "I'm thinking of a master plan, with nothing but sweat inside my hands . . ."

"Excuse me, would you walk me to my truck?" she asked after noticing me doing it for other women that were calling it a night or just out club hopping. "What, your boy ain't ready to leave yet?"

She smiled as I stood up from my stool beside the door.

"No, I just don't want to pull him away from Ms. Thang he over there talking to." She pointed to her son.

"Oh. Yeah, somebody's gonna get laid tonight!" I sang, noticing how much the girl he was talking to was feeling what was in her cup and the game he was running.

"At least one of us is."

Wow. That comment caught me by surprise. "What? No, not you too?" I joked. "But if you're trying to have an after party, just hang around, it's still early."

"No, I'm not trying to do that. But it would be nice to find someone to chill and talk with. I don't think that's going to happen up in here."

"Hey, lady, some of us gotta work and can't afford to sit around partying all night," I responded as I allowed two women dressed in skin-tight short skirts inside.

"I didn't mean nothing by it."

"It's alright, I was just playing anyway. What's your name?"

She stepped to the side so a few more people could enter, before answering.

"Tammy, what's yours, and don't tell me a nick-name. I gave you my real name, so give me yours."

"It's Lord," I lied, smiling hard.

"Is it really?"

"No. I really don't have a nickname that I use, so we don't have an issue there. My name is Assa, you can call me Ace if that's easier to remember."

"I think I can remember Asa just fine, thank you very much."

"Okay, that's good that you can remember that, but it's not my name. It's Assa. A-S-S-A, not A-S-A," I spelled it out for her.

"Oh, I'm sorry. Ace it is then." She laughed.

"It's easy to remember and to say. Y'all just seem

to think I'm saying my own name wrong or something. Say it with me now. As-sa."

"How do people get Ace outta that?"

"I don't fuckin' know. I just let people call me what they want as long as it's respectful."

We kept talking for what seem like an hour. We made each other laugh talking about the way people were dressed or how drunk they were. "What happened to you leaving?"

"Okay, since you're sick of me already, let me get up and go."

"I didn't say all that. I'm actually enjoying you and would like to enjoy more of you." She raised her eyebrows and looked at me sideways. "I didn't mean it like that. I'm not a jump-down-ass nigga, and I try not to fool with that type of female."

"That's good to know." She relaxed again.

"Now, don't get me wrong. I don't look at a female

as a hoe if she set it out on the first date. It's just two grownups knowing what they want at the time, but the key to that is, date."

"Okay. So what do you call a date?"

"What do you like? Tell me and we can finish this conversation then?"

"Really, Assa! You're really gonna ask me, but with a ring on your finger? Are you married?"

"Yes, but believe it or not we broke up over a month ago. And before you tell me you heard this all before, why don't you come back tomorrow night so we can talk about it?"

"I'll think about it." She gathered her things and then went to say her goodbyes to her son before coming back over by me. "Do I still get an escort to my truck?"

"No, you can find it just fine yourself." I had to laugh at the look on her face when I told her that.

"Come on, I was just playing. I couldn't live with myself if something happened to you on my watch."

We walked arm in arm across the street to the parking lot to her black-and-maroon GMC Yukon. She thanked me with a hug before getting in and pulling off with a sexy wave.

My night was going good up until two of Big J's goons got into it with one of the guys off of Thirty-Third Street. I didn't know what it was about, but when the fists started flying, I had to break it up. I tossed the two skinny fools around like kids. I guess Big J didn't like how I was handling his men because he rushed me from behind. I caught his reflection in the mirrors surrounding the dance floor and sent him flying backward into a few more of his wannabe goons with a hard back kick in his fat-ass belly. His guys helped him to his feet, but before anything more could happen a few of the niggas off

Thirty-Third pulled guns. Hey, don't ask me how they got 'em in there; I did my part. There were a few of them already in the spot before I made it in to work.

Remember I'm not strapped, and I'm also not from around these parts, so I wasn't feeling these odds one bit, but I didn't back down. Hell, I couldn't run if I wanted to because I was right smack in the middle of the two groups. But before the lead got to flying a cocky short guy with a mouth full of gold and thick icy rose-gold icy chain draped around his neck stepped up and told them to put the guns away.

"Big boy, if you gotta issue with the way my nigga here doing his job, then you gotta issue with us. You know them fools were trippin' on some drunk shit. He's just trying to make sure we can keep having a good time in this bitch. Now I don't know if y'all got some personal shit going on and don't care, but if you do, then handle that shit someplace else," the man said.

I'd seen the short guy and his clique in the club pretty much every night since I started working there. So I knew they called him Lil Buddy, and the two goons holding the guns were known as, Fat Tee and Big Ray. I was thankful when they stepped in because I wasn't gonna make it on my own. As I told you before, I'm good with my hands and feet, but this ain't that TV shit. I knew I couldn't take on, and win against, six or so niggas that were all trying to show out for Big J and the man himself. But if I had to, I was going to fight until I couldn't anymore.

"Nawl, ain't no shit with us, Lil Buddy. Like you said, I'll catch this clown in the street." He shot me the best menacing look he could muster.

I laughed and shook my head because I really

wanted to make an example out of him. Show the lame he couldn't fight. But not only was this my job, but it was also my friend's place of business, so I held my tongue.

"Okay, that's it for the night, everybody. Thanks to the fools who couldn't act right, we gotta call it a night. But we'll be looking forward to seeing y'all all back here tomorrow," DJ Tone announced. "And let's give it up for Ace to let him know we all feel much safer now that he's here."

I went on and helped Baabie get the club cleared, then helped the DJ load his equipment into his minivan. After Baabie paid and thanked me for the night. I told him that I would be back tomorrow and left him and his few friends to their little after-party. On the way to my car I was reading the messages on my phone and didn't pay attention to the three guys sitting on the steps of the house next door. I had just put my phone away when suddenly I was snatched up from behind. As soon as I felt the angry arms around my neck and chest, I knew who it was right away.

The skinny punk was stronger than I thought, but then his two buddies didn't give me much of a chance to shake him off of me. They threw vicious combinations at my head and body that I had to take because of the hold he had on me. I did my best to toss the punk off me. It wasn't until I spun and slammed him into the trunk of the Caddy that I broke his hold. I turned around quickly, grabbing him by the head with both hands, and commenced to driving my knees into his face a few fast, hard times before letting him fall. I turned toward his guys, who must have been shocked because they stood there a moment too long. I quickly stepped up between them and fed them a few hateful combinations of fist and elbows that dropped one and made the other run back. Once that happened I took off running through the gangway between the house and the club just in case they had guns or more friends somewhere waiting. I didn't run far, just around the house so I could jump in my car when they chased after me. But they didn't come after me. I watched them run across the street and drive off. Then I rushed from my hiding place and got in my car and sped away heading to Angel's for some TLC.

Chapter 12

Club Life Continues

TO MAKE SURE I would be taken more serio-

usly, I went out and bought two black steel retrac-

table batons and two shiny security shields. I

wanted to buy a few black tees with the word

SECURITY across the front and back of them, but

I couldn't find my size. So that evening I dressed in

all black and went to work. When I arrived, Tammy

was in my parking spot waiting on me. I smiled and

pulled in behind her and then turned the Caddy

over to my sister so she could go pick the twins up

from a party at Chuck E. Cheese's.

"Hey, you. I didn't expect to see you again," I said,

walking up to her truck's window.

"I bet you didn't," she said, eyeing my sister as

she drove away in the car. Once she was gone,

Tammy climbed out of her truck wearing a sexy,

tight denim cat suit that showed off her curves very

well. She looked just as good if not better than she

had the night before. Tonight she wore her hair

down in curly micro-braids with just a hint of

makeup. I liked that she knew how to use make-up

to enhance her look and not make it. Some women

believe the more they put on, the better. They be

walking around thinking they look fly, but really

looking like clowns. "Was that her?"

"Who? My wife? Noooo. That was my sister." I

saw she was giving me that look. "For real, you can

talk to her when she come pick me up."

"I believe you. Because if I was your wife I wouldn't just pull off without letting these bitches know that you're mine," she explained, waiting for me to open the door to the club for her.

"I'm curious, how would you do that?"

"Like this." She stepped up and hugged me once we were inside.

"Okay, but some hoes might need a little more to get their minds right. I mean, I hug my sister all the time."

"Oh, wait until we go on that date you promised me."

"I don't remember making that promise, but I'ma make good on it," I agreed. "I have to say again that I'm not a big balla, so make it light on me when you pick the spot you want me to take you."

"I'll do better. I'll take you on the first date, and

you can surprise me with the second."

"Sounds like a plan to me." I excused myself to go check in with Baabie and make a quick walk through the club to see who all was there, then went back to Tammy.

"Mane told me what happened last night after I left."

"And what was that, because a lot happened after you took off."

"Oh, he said that you were kicking ass and taking names," she told me, smiling.

"Not really." I chuckled. "But I made them niggas think twice about just running up on me again." I didn't know which incident she was talking about, but my answer covered them both.

The night was uneventful, which was a good thing. Baabie talked to me about getting me some help. I thought it was a good idea because I couldn't walk through the club and make sure everything was cool once the flood of partygoers came pouring in. He also gave me my props on hooking Tammy.

Over the next few days I saw a lot of Tammy, and by the end of the week I had her cumming and screaming my name bent over the black leather loveseat at her house. I think that was on a Thursday afternoon after I came from my PO visit. Anyway, that night she came to the club to sit and chill with me since it was her last day off from work. Donna's friends came in and saw how close I was with Tammy and called her to come to the club.

As soon as Donna walked through the door I told Tammy who she was. To my surprise Donna didn't say anything to us, but I did find out that she knew a lot of guys in the spot, especially that nigga Big J. When that fool came in and saw her, he had his hands all over her. Donna had him trickin' on her and her friends big-time. I wondered if he was the one she was fuckin' with while I was on lockdown. Hell, if so it would explain why the punk disliked me when he didn't know me. But from the way they were acting with each other, I knew he wasn't.

As the night got going, the crowd grew bigger and wilder. The guy Baabie hired to help me called himself Bear. He was about five foot nine and stocky, and I had to show him how I ran things at the door as well as let him know who's who in the spot, because Baabie had a lot of people that he was cool with and allowed inside no matter what. While I was showing Bear the ropes, I didn't see Donna start fuckin' with Tammy. The next thing I knew Tammy was in my ear telling me to call her if I could when I got off work. Then she left without asking me to walk her to her truck. I was so busy that I just watched her from the door wondering what the hell just happened. A few minutes later Donna came over to me.

"I see your ugly-ass bitch ran off," she slurred, letting me know she's had a nice amount to drink.

"Don't act like that, Donna. You don't want me, and I ain't said shit to you about that bitchboy you got with his hands all over you and shit. So gon with that."

I turned my back on her and went back to checking ID cards at the door. I knew her seeing me with someone else would bother her. I tried my best not to let that happen. Just because she hurt me didn't mean I wanted to see her hurt, and from the look in her eyes, she was. I wanted to tell her to go home, but I didn't want her to make a scene. So I just kept doing what I was doing and staying out of her way.

At the end of the night I helped get the club clear and all that. I didn't have a ride home since my sister had the car.

I called Tammy to come pick me up from work. Not just because I needed a ride, but also because wanted to see where she had run off to and why. Tammy let me know that we were good by kidnapping me for the night. It was the first night I spent with her. All she said to me about her leaving the club the way she did was that my wife was doing too much. Then she told me to leave work at work, her way of telling me she didn't want to talk about her.

In the morning or later that morning depending how you look at it, Tammy took me home to my sister's. When we turned into the parking lot, I immediately noticed the Suburban parked out front of the building.

"Well this is gonna be some bullshit. My wife's here," I told Tammy, shaking my head. "Let me call my sister and see what's she on." I called my sister, and my sister told me she never came over. "I'll call you later after I find out what's going on," I told Tammy, then got out of her truck.

She got out and called me back to give her a hug. I did, and she got back in her truck and pulled off. That's when I noticed Donna was sitting out there. She quickly pulled off in the Suburb-an. I hoped she wasn't going to fuck with Tammy, but what could I do if she was? My sister had the keys to the Caddy. But by the time I crossed the parking lot just as Donna was turning into it, she stopped right beside me, window down, crying and asking if we could talk.

"What is it to talk about, Donna?"

"Us, our family."

Oh, now she wanted to think about our family. It took her to see my broke ass with another woman for her to know I was good enough for her. I let her try to explain why she did what she did and how she didn't want me to go but she didn't want to look weak.

"I hear all of that, but I'm still doing the same shit. I'm not with this getting put out shit. So if you really want our family, then okay. But I ain't coming back until I got a real job or a better one." I looked her right in the eyes and hit her with, "I don't want you to have to take care of no grown-ass man."

So, no, I didn't move back in with her—not right away anyway. But I did start back talking to her on the phone, which led to me taking her out to a nice place to eat for her birthday, that ended up with us in a cheap motel having wild, uncut birthday sex.

Chapter 13

Donna

NO, DON'T NOBODY GOTTA tell me. I
know I was wrong for what I did to Ray after all he
went through to pull me out of the hole I was in
when he came home. I didn't mean for it to go this
far. Lord knows I never wanted to push my husband
into the arms of that bitch I saw him with. I can
admit I was jealous. The bitch looked just the way I
had imagined she would when they told me about
them being all hugged up together at the club he

was working at. She was smaller, looked younger, and had a body like she didn't have kids or maybe just one. Anyway, fuck her! I have his daughter, and I know that because of her Ray will do whatever for us. I don't give a fuck what you believe, but it's not all about money with me. Well, not with my husband. Ray just got me used to living a certain way before he went to prison, and he was a different person. I want that life back!

Like I said, I know I put myself in the position I'm in with him, and I'ma get myself out of it.

"Ma! Our daddy here," Autumn announced, running into the kitchen excitedly.

"Well go let him in." I was just as excited as my baby was that he was there. When he walked in dressed in black Dickie cargo pants, with a black long-sleeve T-shirt, and black Timberlands, I knew he would be going to work at that punk-ass club after he left here. I wanted to ask him to take the night off, but how would that sound after I called him a broke-ass nigga to his face? "Bae, could you see what's wrong with the washer while you're here? It's not draining right."

"Yeah, okay, I'ma do it now," he told me, putting Autumn down off his back. "Who wanna come help me fix the washer?" he asked the boys.

"I do, I do!" the two young ones sang. They loved to do things with him, and I loved to watch my husband teaching them things. Ray has not once treated my kids as anything less than his own.

"Hey, what you in here cooking that's smelling so good?" he asked on his way down to the basement where the laundry room was.

"Lasagna and garlic rolls. It'll be ready in a few if you got time to eat?"

"Yeah, I got time. Fix me a plate. This shouldn't

take long. It's probably just clogged up in the drain hose," he told me, and then him and the boys walked out the back door.

I got busy with the food while talking to my sister on the phone. That's when I heard my oldest daughter calling for me as she rushed into the kitchen. "What is it, Danae?"

"It's a white lady at the door with the police."

"What?" I hurried to the door to see who it was.

"Are you Donna Jones?" the woman asked, holding a clipboard.

"Yeah. What's this about?"

"I'm from the child welfare office." She pushed her way inside of my house with the police in tow.

"Danae, go get your dad, now!" I called my mother to come over just in case I needed her.

"What's this about?" Ray asked the woman once him and the boys made it back upstairs and saw

143

the police.

"Sir, I'm going to need you to calm down and have a seat next to your wife!" one of the officers ordered, getting in his face.

"Bae, just come here. These muthafuckas looking for reason to arrest somebody."

Two officers stood over us as the old bitch and another questioned the kids one at a time in the kitchen.

"This some bullshit," said Ray to the officers.

"This has to be a prank call or something. We love our children and would never do anything to hurt them," I told the officer, wishing she was done with her interview of the kids and looking around the house.

"Well that's what we are here to find out, ma'am. I'm sure Mrs. Stebbins will be in here to answer any questions you have soon."

"Can she even talk to them without one of us there with them?" Ray asked, addressing the officers.

"In a matter such as this she can. Now save your questions for her, or be cited for disorderly. Your choice," the officer threatened him.

"Bae, let's just wait on her. Don't give them a reason to lock you up," I pled, trying my best to calm him down.

"I overheard you on the phone with your mom, was it?"

"Yeah, she's on her way here. Why?"

"Do you believe she will be willing to take temporary custody of the children?"

"Temporary custody for what!" Ray snapped.

"Please don't make this hard," she warned us. "I haven't found reason enough at this time to lock either of you up on charges, but I do have issues with the home that you're going to need to address before I return the children to you," Mrs. Stebbins explained.

"What's wrong with the house? It's clean as fuck in here," Ray snapped, looking around bewildered.

"Well, Mr. Jones, for one, there aren't enough bedrooms. Two, the bags of dirty clothes that are sitting in the kitchen, and there's a window out in the back bedroom. Those are just a few."

My mother and sister made it there just in time to get the kids so the bitch could get the hell outta my face.

"I was just working on the washer when you got here so we can wash the clothes. And the boys didn't tell me they broke the window in their room until just a minute ago. Ma'am, you don't gotta do this. I'll have all that stuff fixed first thing in the morning," my husband pled with her.

"I'm sorry. Someone from my office will be getting in touch with you within a week. Until then, I'm removing the children from this unsafe home."

My mother took my babies to her house so the coldhearted bitch wouldn't take them away to wherever they put kids. She told Ray and I that we couldn't go anywhere near them until the investigation was over. I did my best to explain to my kids that this was just some type of misunderstanding and they would be back home soon

After everybody was gone, I pulled myself together enough to call Mary. I asked her to have her mother, who worked for child welfare, to find out what she could about what was going on and who made the bogus call on us. Mary hung up and got right on it. Ray had called and told Baab that he wouldn't be coming in to work and stayed there with me. I could see the hurt in his eyes as my tears fell harder. This was not how I planned for the night to go.

Chapter 14

Shattered Dreams

"**I NEED EVERYONE** I fuck with to be on the same page, and know that I wouldn't ask y'all to do nothing I wouldn't do for you or with you. I want us all to have pockets full of money and nice whips an' shit. The only way I know how to make that happen is if we all stay focused on gettin' that cash. So you're all the way in or all the way out; ain't no halfway shit. All I ask is that you try to cop more than you did the last time. We're tryin' to come up, not go down, so if this ain't what you're on, then you don't need to be here." I was addressing a small group of young thugs I knew from the hood who wanted to get down with me. They all seemed to be okay with my terms, so I opened my new spot and got down to business.

Yeah, I got back in them streets. Why? Because I didn't have a realistic choice. I was a convicted felon who had never held down a job for longer than a few months, so no one was quick to give me the type of loan I needed at the time. So what else was I to do when the bitch took the kids last year? To get them back she told Donna that we had to move into a bigger house, one with at least five bedrooms because the boys couldn't be mixed with the girls, nor could the older kids be in with the younger ones. That's just fucked up. When I was growing up, I sometimes shared a room with five or six others of all ages and genders. As you know, we were barely keeping the roof of the three-bedroom we were in over our heads.

Everyone knows a single-family home costs more in rent and everything to maintain. She also told us we needed to get new appliances. What the fuck! The stuff we had worked just fine. Well, anyway, that and holding my distraught wife as she cried herself to sleep is what broke me. So if you think I was wrong for going back to selling that soft white flake to get my family back together again, then you live a much better life than me.

So I bet the next thing you wanna know is why I was still out there after we got the kids back. Because I still had to maintain it all, and to be real with you, I was just tired of being broke. I allowed Donna to dress the house the way she wanted it. She got all new everything just about. All the kids' bedrooms had their own TVs and games. The kitchen had matching stainless steel appliances. We bought a new washer and dryer set and two deep freezers. You name it; she bought it for the house. Oh yeah, and all new clothes for everybody. Because of the issue with the kids, Donna missed too many days of work and lost her job working with my cousin. But she got a job as a teacher at a childcare center to help out, but her checks only covered things for her and the kids. Now if that's still not reason enough, remember, I'm a felon.

I had a plan to stack enough money so we could keep the house running the way it was so I could open up a used car sales and repair shop. I've always loved cars, and I knew that I could keep a roof over our heads and food on the table doing what I loved. In fact, my uncle Eddie had agreed to take me to buy my first stock of used cars. I also wanted to buy a building so Donna could open her own childcare center. I know that sounds like a lot, but I was trying to do it all at once. I planned to bounce every new venture off of the last one once it was up and running good.

I had just finished with the last of my runs when Eddie called. "Where your ass at, Nephew? Me and your auntie ready to ride out."

"I'm on my way to you now," I answered while counting out the money I planned to spend at the auction, I locked the rest away in one of the two digital safes I kept under my bed. Then I rushed out and jumped in my red 1998 Ford Crown Vic sitting on chrome 22-inch rims. I stormed it down Thirtieth Street until I reached my aunt and uncle's home on Twenty-Eighth and Wright. They came right out of the house when they heard the deep thundering bass from the four 12-inch subwoofers in my trunk.

"If you don't turn that shit down, I'ma have to take it for a joyride," Eddie joked. "Pull it around back and park in the gate so won't nobody fuck with it."

"If they do, then I'ma make these Murder Mob niggas live up to their name." I told him but got back in the car and did as he said.

We drove down to Illinois in his 2005 light gold GMC pickup. He got me there early enough for me to scope out all of the cars I wanted to bid on. They were also there trying to find a car for their daughter who had just totaled her small SUV a few days before. So on the lot we went our separate ways. I found a few vehicles I wanted and then went inside with all the other dealers on the show-room floor.

When the bidding started, it was so loud in the room I could barely understand what the fast-talking guy was saying. There were three lines of vehicles going at once. I stayed running from one lane to another. When it was all over I'd only bought two of the cars out of the ten I had my eyes on, a 2002 maroon Ford Taurus, and a 1998 Jeep Cherokee. But I took home five vehicles in all. I decided the Ford was for Donna to replace the Dodge Sebring that was stolen from behind our house.

Yeah, one morning she was letting the car warm up to take the kids to school, when someone jumped in it and pulled off. When we got it back, it was banged up, and she didn't want it anymore. Even after I told her I could fix it, she said she just wouldn't feel safe in it anymore. So she got rid of it and had been driving my 1995 black-and-silver Chevy Tahoe ever since. I wanted my baby back. Yeah, we still had the old Suburban, plus I owned a full-size Ford custom van that I had bought because I like vans and it fit the size of our family.

Anyways, once I got the vehicles all back to Milwaukee, I parked them on the vacant lot across from the garage behind my mother's house, then went to work in the hood trying to make back the money I had spent on them. I was so excited, I didn't sleep. Donna was upset, but my hypes loved it, so fuck it. I had go with what paid the bills. I knew she would get over it once I gave her the car.

First thing in the morning, I went to work on the vehicles with the help of my Uncle Curt. We gave them all tune-ups and oil changes and did any repairs that needed to be done before I put them out there. We had a blown motor in the Taurus, which was the car Donna picked out for herself like I knew she would. But either way it was off the market for now. I sold a gray Toyota to my Uncle Doc for like $850 as is. The jeep went to a woman for her daughter for $1,600, a small Chevy pickup went to one of my mother's friends for $1,100 and the Dodge Neon sold for $2,200. The best part was I sold them in about three days for a grand total of $5,000. After subtracting the money I spent buying them and the money I paid my uncle for his help, I had profited $2,700. I didn't think that was bad, plus all my customers told their friends about me. So I reinvested, and now I was one step closer to my dream coming true.

I put a motor in the Ford but ending up selling it because Donna had picked out a gold Chrysler concord out my second bunch of vehicles. She kept that for little over a year before someone caused her to run into a tree one snowy morning as she was returning home from dropping the kids off at school. That was quickly replaced by a 2002 Dodge Durango that I put a lot of money into to make her happy and safe. I had it custom painted white rose and put chrome 22-inch rims on it, that I later had to take off because she didn't like the way the truck felt when she drove it. I install-led a nice sound system just so I wouldn't hear her mouth about it later. Now you would think she would be happy with her truck, but, no, she wanted a car as well. So I gave her an icy-blue Nissan Maxima for her birthday. I was actually gonna give it to her for our anniversary, but the police fucked that up when they raided the house where I had it hidden from her at.

That shit was crazy. Donna called me just as I was picking up my 1984 red-and-orange Chevy Monte Carlo. I had it fully customized with the word TAPOUT in the back window.

"Bae, where you at?"

"I'm just picking up TAPOUT from Frank's, why?" I asked as I did a burnout for some young boys who gave me props on the car.

"The police just called me and asked me about a light blue Maxima at a house they raided on Eighteenth Street. Do you know anything about that?"

"How in the hell did they call you?" I made a U-turn on Capital heading to the spot where the car was parked. "Fuck that, can you meet me there? I need to find out what's going on with Lil Buddy because that's his place."

"I'm pulling up there now. Bae, I think these the feds. It's a bunch of black trucks out here. I'm supposed to talk to a detective when I get here. So what do you want me to do?"

"Just talk to them and try to find out as much as you can about what's going on. The car is yours. I was gonna give it to you as a surprise, but that's fucked up now."

WIFE

I ended the call as soon as I turned on the block. I parked behind her truck and then got out and went to explain to the cops that I'd parked the car there because the guy that lived there was a good friend of the family. When they asked about the drugs and money they had found in the house, I told them I didn't know what they were talking about and that it was none of my business what the people that lived in the lower unit of the house did. I didn't know them. All of which was the truth.

That was how she got the car, and also the first real hit I took since I got back in the game. You know what they say, one step forward and two steps back when you're trying to get outta them streets. All because of the police's dumb luck, I had to hustle even harder to get back up what was taken. Anyway, Donna had her sister with her, so she drove her truck home and Donna drove the car.

I just drove around the city for a while to clear my head, because I had to make a whole lot shake in drought season.

Chapter 15

The Flower in the Night

WELL, I HAD TO hit the highway and fall back on moving the bags out there with my niggas. Doing this was how I made it through the drought and got my whole team back out on the streets. I wish I could say life was good, but things with my wife had gotten a little rocky. Donna had been crying about me being out of town and staying weeks at a time. She thought I was out cheating on her with a girl upstate. This was far from the truth. I hadn't been with another woman since we got back together the last time. But Donna had been lying about her whereabouts.

Once she told me that she was with her sister, Tameka, when I knew she wasn't because I had just seen her sister and her mother out at the store. When I called her out on it she told me that she meant to say Mary, and blamed it on them drinking. I let her have that. It was things like that running through my head, along with how she never seemed to answer the phone right away when I called her. It was always that her phone wasn't with her, or some shit like that. But when I was home with her it never left her sight. I was thinking while I was working on my Tahoe at the garage one night.

I had just set out the tools I needed to replace the truck's floodlights, when a crackhead I knew from around the way walked up asking me if I had any drugs.

"Man, you know ain't nothing moving around here!" I got up in his face so he knew I was serious. "You ain't gonna like if I gotta tell you again!"

"Boss man, I don't mean no disrespect." He held up his hands, holding a shopping bag in one. "It's my birthday, and I'm tryin' to cop a lil something and find me a bitch with a mean head game so I can get blowed both ways. Feel me?" He sat the bag down and started pulling things out of it to show me. He was still trying to get something out of me. "Man, I know you can use this shit here. A nigga can never have enough toiletries."

"Here, I'ma give you $20 for everything. Take it or leave it." I pulled out a small wad of cash and peeled off two bills for him.

"It's all good, boss." He accepted the money, looked at it, and said, "Hey, you know you gave me an extra ten spot, right?" He held up the money so I could see it.

"Yeah, I know. You said it was your birthday, right, so happy b-day, nigga." He thanked me then went in search of what he really wanted.

I took a good look through the bag to see if there was anything good I could use in it because you never know what you're getting when you make deals with a crackhead. To my surprise everything was new and still in its unopened packaging. Besides toiletries, there was an at-home DNA testing kit and also a home drug testing kit in the bag. I tossed the bag in my trunk and then slid under it to finish what I was there to do. After about ten minutes or so, I heard a light female voice.

"Mister? Excuse meee, sir!" she sang.

I wasn't ignoring her; I just didn't know she was talking to me. When I slid from under the trunk I

found a short pretty woman standing there dressed
in tight-fitting Coogi jeans and a matching hoodie.
She seemed surprised to see me as well. I was
thinking it was another hype trying to sell me some
more bullshit. "What's up?" I scanned the alley
thinking it might be some kinda set up.

"Can you put this battery in my car for me? It just
stopped, and I gotta go to work tonight."

"Sure. Where's your car?" She pointed to a black
Chrysler 300M. "Damn, I didn't see it there," I
admitted.

"That's not good. You gotta be on point around
here, but I'm not on nothing but trying to get my car
fixed," she told me with a smile.

"I'm not worried one bit." I flashed her a friendly
smile. "Do it start at all, or do I gotta push it over
here?" The car was only about ten feet or so away,
but it was raining and dark out. I needed it closer to

the light.

"No, I let it coast that far before it stopped. But you look pretty strong, so I'll steer while you push."

"Why do you get the easy part?" I joked as we walked over to her car.

"Because I'm paying you to do a job, that's why." She smiled. "I hope you can do it. The guy at AutoZone didn't know where it was."

"He lied to you, Ms. Lady, because he didn't wanna take all this stuff off to get to it." I pulled out a small flashlight and showed her where it was under the hood. "See there, it go right there."

"Okay . . . I see it. Can you do it? I mean, really, do you know what you're doing?"

"What, you don't trust me? Wow. You made me stop working on my own shit and push this damn car down the alley in the rain to have second thoughts?"

"No, it's not like that . . . You just don't seem like you work on cars for real, that's all."

"Whatever. Just step in there out of the rain and let me work." I started unhooking stuff. "Where's the new one?"

"On the floor in the back," she answered, then went back to talking on the phone she held in her hand the whole time.

I guess it was so if something happened to her the other person on the line could call the police. Kinda smart, I guess. It only took me a few minutes to put the battery in.

"All done."

"How much do I owe you?"

"You know what? It's on me. All I want you to do is think of me when you decide to buy a new car. I buy, sell, and repair cars."

"Okay, I can do that. Do you have a card or

anything? What's your name?"

"No, I don't got a card, but you can have my number." I gave her my work cell phone number. "My name is spelled A-S-S-A, Assa, or you can just call me Ace if it's easier to remember."

"Your wife ain't gonna trip on me calling you, is she?" she asked, noticing my ring.

"Not unless you call me for something other than the things I told you I do, but I'm sure you got a man somewhere that won't let that happen."

"Yeah, right. If I had a man I wouldn't be down here stuck in the fuckin' alley by myself."

My cell beeped letting me know I had a text. It was from one of my guys trying to re-up before it got too late. I didn't know how many times I had to tell people that it was never too late to get money. When it called I was coming, day or night. Rain or shine.

"Well, I'ma be looking for your call. It's time for me to get to my other job."

"Whatever, you know that was your wife telling you to come in the house."

"No, it wasn't, and stop pickin'. This my mother's house. So the woman you seen coming out of here is not my wife, and why you so worried about her anyway?"

"I'm just weighing my chances," she flirted, then got in her car. She tapped her horn as she drove away.

I slid back under my truck and finished the lights so I could go get the money I had online, plus I had to go to work at the club. My cell beeped again. This time it was her telling me her name was Mica and to save her number. I don't know, why but I did. Maybe it was the cool vibe I got from her or the way she fit in them jeans. Maybe a bit of both. Time would tell.

~ ~ ~

For the next few weeks, I was seeing Mica a lot. It wasn't on no hookup shit. It was all about her piece of shit 300M. Yeah, she flirted openly with me, but I held strong to my commitment to Donna. I was feeling Mica, I can't lie, but I just couldn't act on it, even though Donna was tripping hard on me. She would find a reason to cuss me out one minute about being out at all hours of the night hustling, then tell me she needed money for all type of shit the next. What the fuck! Oh, I forgot to mention that she quit her job, so it was all on me again.

"I'm not a fuckin' airhead, Ray. You sell weight, nigga. It ain't no reason for you to be out the way you do, except for you to be fucking some bitch!"

"Donna, I was doing the same shit when you met me and keeping the same fuckin' hours. I'm not one

170

that thinks this shit is forever.

The niggas that do is the ones doing stupid shit like shutting down at eight and nine o' clock. I'm not trying to be out here for too much longer. I don't gotta lie to you!" I argued. "You know what, get your shit on, you're coming with me tonight so you can see just how much work I be putting in." She must have thought I was bluffing because she just stood there. "I said get your shit!" That made her see that I was serious. She put on her shoes and jacket.

We hit the streets. I allowed her to witness just how I was out in traffic when I was doing my thang at night.

"Bae, can we stop and get something to eat? I haven't eaten since this morning," she asked once we were in my car.

"Yeah, it gotta be something with a drive-thru because I got a lot of niggas waiting on me."

The night had to be one of my best nights all week in the city. By the time things had slowed down it was past three in the morning. Donna didn't trip on me for a long time after witnessing that. And before you ask, I did slow down a bit and spent more time with her and the kids. I took them to the movies and out for family dinners. I even ordered takeout and chilled at home with my phones off, leaving my guys, Rome and Mane, to take care of things.

For about two months, things were good between us, until one night after we went to bed. This girl Rome was messing around with came knocking on my door. She must have thought he lived there because she saw his car out front of the house more than once. To make a long story short, Donna didn't believe me about the bitch, so I left and went to my safe house. It was a room I rented from my uncle for times like this really. Most of my clothes were there anyway because Donna had put me out of the house one too many times in the past. I'm not with that, and the only thing that kept me from leaving her was the promise I made to our kids, and my PO, who I only had a few more weeks to deal with before my three years was done.

Remember that DNA testing kit I bought from crackhead Willie? I used it on our daughter, Autumn. It wasn't that I had doubts that she was mine, because she was the spitting image of Pooh, my oldest from my first marriage. Yeah, I've been married twice, but Donna was to be my last. I wasn't going for strike three. Even though she was doing a lot of things I had strong issues with, like drinking, smoking weed, lying about her whereabouts, and spending more. There was so much money unaccounted for it was a shame. Nice amounts of drugs were missing. That shit was crazy, too, but still none of that was the reason I tested my child. I just was curious and wanted to see if the kit worked for real, and put unrecognized doubts to rest. You know the saying, "Mama's baby, Daddy's maybe."

One night I was chillin' with the kids. Autumn had fallen asleep on the couch curled up with our little dog Roxie. Donna was down in the bedroom doing something on the laptop. I went out to the van, got the kit, got a swab from it, and went back inside and swabbed the little girl. Then I did the same thing to myself. When I got back to the safe house I sent it in to the lab, along with the $120 processing fee.

I used that address and my personal email address so it would come right to me. A week later I received the life-changing results. You guessed right, Autumn wasn't mine. There was another saying that I grew up hearing, "If you don't want to get hurt, then don't look for it." And that shit hurt. I checked online to see if it was a misprint. I even went out to Walgreens and bought two more kits and tested both Pooh and my little brother. All was on point. I was crushed. I love that little girl. I wondered if Donna knew the truth or not because she was just getting out of a relationship with her son's father when we got together. But then we had been together like a year before she got pregnant, so now I knew she cheated on me. It might've been some get-back shit she was on after seeing me with one of my exes. Who knows?

I shed some tears in the dark alone in my room. I let the day turn into night and then pulled myself together and went down to the club where Donna's mother worked as a barmaid. I allowed my mother-in-law's cougar friends, sitting around the bar, to get me drunk in hopes of getting me home with one of them or some shit. Now remember, I'm not much of a drinker, so you know it didn't take much to get me wasted. Mom called T-Bay and Moe to come get me. When they got there, Moe took my car, and T-Bay and his wife took me home with them.

Bro thought it was funny to see me like that. I cried to him and his wife about it all in the car. Now they are drinkers, and T-Bay loved himself some beer, so he stopped at the store to get him some for the night. I went in with him. Fuck it, I bought my mother's go-to drink, Korbel, and downed the whole bottle right in the store. I was so out of it, I mean a nigga couldn't see straight. I don't understand how people like to feel like that. Anyway, I took off walking down the street. Bro was chasing after me. Him and his wife were laughing as they tried to get me back in the car. That's when, from outta nowhere, some nigga rushed me. I beat the breaks off of the punk and then left him lying face down in the dirty snowbank that lined the sidewalk.

T-Bay grabbed me from behind to keep me from continuing to beat the unconscious man. I tossed bro off of me and then went after him thinking he was another punk trying to do something to me. If it wasn't for his wife screaming my name for me to stop, I would've hurt him too. They got me back in the car. I think I passed out in the backseat, because the next thing I knew they were helping me outta the car. Once they got me inside their home, I passed out on the kitchen floor. Big bro didn't bother trying to wake me or pick me up. I don't know if it was from fear that I may come at him again, or that I was just too heavy.

The next morning when I woke up I had a lot of cleaning up to do. I guess I had gotten sick in the middle of the night, throwing up in my drunk heartbroken haze. I also did a lot of apologizing for my actions the night before after they told me what happened.

They were very understanding. They both thought it would be best if I didn't tell Donna about my plan on leaving her.

"Bruh, you're gonna love that baby the same way as you always have because that's just you. I know it hurts like a muthafucka. Hell, I hurt for you, but that's still your child," T-Bay told me over his morning beer.

"All she know is you, Assa. Don't take that away from that baby. You shouldn't punish her for the sins of her mother. Just give the relationship some space until you get your mind right," Koco explained while washing the dishes from breakfast.

By the time Moe made it there to pick me up in my car, I was feeling better from my hangover. I was glad he didn't talk much after giving me shit about all of the things I didn't remember doing the night before. He dropped himself off at home, and I climbed behind the wheel and drove to the garage and traded the Crown Vic for my Tahoe. I needed the deep hard bass and uncut lyrics of Alley Boy, Yo Gotti, and Slim Thug to help me get to the money I missed over almost two days.

It was mid-afternoon when I made my mind up to take the advice I was given and give the relation-ship with Donna a break. I wasn't going to turn my back on the kids, nor was I going to stop paying the bills at the house. But I just couldn't stay married to her if she knew about Autumn and just didn't tell me. That shit was just dirty as hell. I did plan on talking to her about it. I believed I could read her like a book, and I was going to treat her like I would some nigga in the streets when we did talk, instead of my wife of ten years.

I finished my rounds and ended up at Mica's place just to hang out and talk. I didn't want to be alone, so we watched a few movies that I had picked up from one of my trips to the Windy City. She was a good listener and didn't press me about what was really going on with me. I liked that about her because it's just what a nigga needed right then.

Chapter 16

Donna

"BLACKIE, I'M TELLING YOU, something is really going on with Ray. I know him like I know myself and this shit he been on lately, it's more than a bitch he fuckin'."

"Donna, are you really sure about that?" Deidra spoke between smoking a blunt from Ray's stash that he had left at the house a week ago.

"Yeah, this is something more. I can feel it." Deidra passed the blunt to me then crawled to the foot of the bed. I met Deidra a few months back through my sister, Neek. I'm not gay, and I'm married. I just like the way she gives me the time I crave, and, yes, the sex is great too. I'd always been a little curious, even more so now that Neek came out to the family. But this isn't all that serious. I'm just having fun with a friend. I learned the hard way that I couldn't fool around with a man like this because they keep trying to take my husband's place. Like that time when Vince pushed up on me at the club where my mother works knowing good and well that I was there with my husband. A bitch was scared to death when Vince got up in Ray's face. His skinny ass didn't have a chance with Ray. If it wasn't for my mom I might've lost his ass to the system again. After that night I cut all ties with that lovesick nigga and did my best to be a better wife to my husband, on top of being the down-ass bitch he needed me to be while he did what he had to do to take care of home.

"Hell, do you think he know about me?" she asked, removing her black du-rag and T-shirt.

"No! How could he when he ain't been paying no mind lately? The kids are the only ones that really has seen him lately." I took another puff of the strong weed.

"Yeah, that still might be the reason he ain't been around . . . But enough talking about that nigga. Right now you're my bitch, and a nigga needs some of that good-good." She began skillfully fingering my sweet spot, turning me on the way she knew she could.

"Ooooh shit, bae, that feels good. Make me cum. Yes, make this pussy cum for you," I moaned as she made me do just that over and over again once she added her long tongue and big black strap-on into the mix. It was over for me.

On my way home after my little fuckfest, I return-ed one of many missed calls from Ray. "Bae, you called? I couldn't answer because I was in the doctor's office with Neek and my phone had died in my purse. I didn't know it until now," I lied. I had to remember to call my sister and put her up on game, just in case he called her.

"Whatever. Where you at now?"

"On my way home. I should be there in like five minutes. Is something wrong?"

"I don't know yet, but we'll talk more when you get to the house. I'm on my way there as soon as I leave this gas station."

I didn't like the tone of his voice. It kinda made me wonder if he knew something about me and Deidra. "Okay, bae, love you."

"Me too."

WIFE

He hung up before I could address that weak-ass response. It wasn't like him not to confess his love. I tell you, if a bitch wasn't worried before, she is now.

~ ~ ~

Waiting for Ray to pull up, I saw Deidra ride past on her way to open the gay club that she and her sister owned down the street from my house. I texted her and told her not to call me until I called her because I had to deal with my husband. Then I called Neek to cover my ass for all of the lies that I'd been feeding him. I was still on the phone with Neek when he pulled in behind me. He was driving the van I bought him. Sure, it was his money, but it was the thought that counted. Anyways, what's his is mine and what's mine is mine. I went and bought the van a week after he showed it to me and said he was thinking about getting it to replace the one he had given his sister. The first red flag that something was wrong was that I didn't hear the bass from the system in the van when he pulled up. I got out of my truck and climbed into the van with him. I noticed was he was looking good, freshly shaved, dressed in a gray-and-red Akoo outfit with his rose gold icy watch and matching bracelet that set the look off just right. The next thing I noticed was the song he was playing low. It was "Nobody" by Kern, and last, I noticed my photo displayed on the screen of the TV in the dash.

"Neek, let me call you back." I ended the call, letting him know it was my sister at the same time. "I didn't know you still had that picture." I pointed to the screen and smiled, he didn't.

"Why wouldn't I?" He paused the song, and I knew this was bad. I'ma kill him if he tells me that he got a bitch prego. "Donna, the way you answer what I'm about to ask you has a lot riding on it."

"What's wrong? What is it?" I interrupted.

"Just let me talk. This shit is hard enough as it is." He turned in the seat so he was facing me. I could see the tears burning in his eyes. I turned in my seat so we would be face-to-face. "Is Autumn mine? Don't get mad, just answer the question."

"Ray, yeah, she yours. Where is this coming from all of a sudden?"

"Do you honestly believe that in your heart?"

"Yes. Tell me where this is coming from."

"Well, that's not what the test said."

Oh my God! Noo, this couldn't be happening. "What test, Ray? You took my baby and had her tested without telling me?"

"No, I tested her myself, when she was sleeping. I used one of them home kits, and before you ask, I tested Pooh and Ville, just to be sure the shit

187

worked."

Real tears came to my eyes because I knew this wasn't just some made-up bullshit and that I was about to lose my husband. He already had another place where he lived when we argued or got stressed out with each other. "Why would you do that? If you had doubts, all you had to do was ask me and . . ."

"I didn't have doubts. I just tested her because I had the kit lying around and wanted to see if it worked. That's it."

"What now, Ray? What now!" My tears were coming down hard now, and my chest hurt so bad it felt like somebody ripped my heart out. "Ray, I need you! You're my husband and you're all she knows. I love you and need you in our life."

"I know, and I love y'all too. I don't want to take shit away from her. No matter what happens with us, she's mine." Tears were racing down his face. "I was there for her when she was born. I held her when she couldn't sleep at night!"

I reached out for his hand, but he pulled it away.

"Bae, I didn't tell you this before because I didn't want you mad at me, but Mack's mother seen me and Autumn out one day at Pick N Save and asked if she was her granddaughter, talking about she looked just like the rest of his kids. So I put my doubts to rest and had her tested. It came back negative. I promise to God, on my life, I wasn't with nobody else! Please believe me?"

"Then how did she get here, Donna! Because this is legit!" He showed me his phone that played a video of the test results. "I was just gonna send this to your phone, but I needed to be looking in your face when I asked you this shit."

"Baby, please, don't leave us. I can't live without

you! I promise I'll get myself together and stop cussing and fighting with you. I'll go to counseling like you asked. Anything, Rayson, just please don't go," I begged hard.

"I don't know what to do. This shit hurts bad, Donna. I can't tell my family this shit. Nobody! I feel like a fuckin' fool! But my heart is still here with y'all." He shook his head, drying his face with his hands. That's when I noticed he wasn't wearing his ring. "I just, I just need to be away from you to think right now I gotta go." He turned away from me in his seat.

"Nooo, wait, let's talk."

"Donna, I'm all talked out for right now. Just go in the house. I'm going somewhere to clear my head."

I saw it was no use talking to him right now, so I got out of the van and watched my husband drive away. I honestly didn't know if I was going to see him again. There was no amount of pussy or food that would fix this shit I was in with him. All I could think of was that Mack must have done something with the test so his ugly-ass wife wouldn't find out and leave his ass. I went in the house and locked myself in my bedroom. I did some more crying before I called Neek to come over because I didn't wanna be alone with the loaded gun that I kept in my nightstand. I don't know, but I do know I'ma get some answers and I ain't giving up my husband to another bitch. "Oh my God, what did I do?"

Chapter 17

She Made the Bed

AFTER DAYS OF THINKING, stressing, trying to decide if I should stay or go, I did something I hadn't done since the night when the kids were taken from us because Donna had threatened a teacher and the bitch called CPS to get back at her: I got down on my hands and knees and prayed. When I was done, I called my auntie and asked her to come with me to file for a divorce. My aunt was sad that I had decided this was the best way for me, but she knew it was what I had to do. After something like that, how can a man stay with a woman? I knew I'd fallen outta love with Donna and wasn't no going back to it from here. I told her that I would always be there for her and the kids, and that I would still help pay the bills at the house as long as she didn't have a man. Not that I wanted to control her or her house. I didn't give a fuck who she was fuckin' anymore. I was just not helping her if she start dealing with someone else because it wouldn't be my responsibility, it'd be his. So she'd better get someone that was just as good as I was or better, because the first I heard of another would be the last red cent I shelled

out to her. I don't believe a nigga could be no realer than that.

I tell you, the single life wasn't what it used to be. I guess I'd just gotten use to the married life. I saw the kids almost every day when I came over to drop Autumn off to school. I had to start sitting on the bus stop with the two younger boys after some bullies robbed them and one of their friends for their iPods and games. The punks even took the new shoes off of their friend's feet, and it was his birthday. So after I tracked them down from the info about the car they were driving, I put a few of my young goons on it. They made sure the punks never fucked with the boys again. Hey, when you're a street nigga, you handle things in the street. Some call it street justice; us in the ghettos call it life.

Anyway, I didn't see the two older children unless I was dropping them off money for something or giving them rides from school when I caught them standing at the city bus stop waiting. And last-ly, Donna. We talked every day about something. Plus

I still called her to let her know when I was about to
hit the highway to handle my business outta state
or upstate, and I called her once I came back. This
was mostly done out of habit because I also called
and told Mica the same. But I took Donna out on a
few friendly dates, so we could talk about the kids
and things face-to-face. Plus I didn't like eating
alone all the time. I wasn't trying to lead her to
believe we were anything more than friends. Yeah,
I did end up having sex with her once or twice, but
that was because she had called begging for it,
talking about she needed to be touched in "only the
way" I knew how. Okay, fuck it. I wanted to fuck her
too. But I cut all of that out once I got serious with
Mica.

"Daddy, come get me!" My oldest daughter de-
manded, crying over the phone.

"I'm on my way. What's wrong?"

"My mama trying to fight me because her and Rick got into it!"

Just when I thought the chapter with my soon-to-be ex-wife, Donna, was over, my Pooh called with this. "Where she at now? Put her ass on the phone!" I was pissed the fuck off that she was letting her good-for-nothing husband come between her and her child.

This wasn't like Peachee. When we were together she wouldn't have done nothing like that. I guess the nigga had beaten the self-esteem out of her.

"I don't know. I had to hit her with something to get her off of me. Then I ran in the bathroom and locked the door."

What the fuck! "Okay, I'll be there in a minute." I could hear her mother hollering something at my daughter, but I couldn't make out the words.

WIFE

When I picked my daughter up from her mother's, her mother was too upset to stop me. I didn't waste time trying to find out what went down. I just took my baby and went back to my place. You know the way I lived, so my place wasn't right for a teenage girl or any kid. So I called on the only person that I thought I could count on to make sure my baby was good. You guessed right if you guessed Donna.

She welcomed my baby into her home with open arms. Donna had always treated her as one of her own. Pooh even called her "Momma" like the rest of the kids. My baby liked to be there because she could be a kid like she was, instead of taking care of her younger siblings, and most of all so she could be with me. Even though she was living with Donna, I wasn't. I did, however, spend more nights there with them because of her. I slept in other parts of the house at first, but then after seeing how happy all the kids were for all of us to be together, I gave in and played house once again. Yeah, our divorce was still in motion and I had no plans on calling it off. I was only planning on keeping my baby until things cooled down and got back right between her and her mother. But then one day Peachee went and allowed her husband to take Pooh from school. I don't know what the punk was thinking when he decided it was a good idea to choke my baby and scratch up her face and neck. Yeah, when I got to my baby all I saw was red. I guess that hoe-ass nigga thought I was sweet or something. That I would let him get away with doing some shit like that.

I'ma make a long story shorter for you. Pooh had just got to her cell phone that they had taken away from her before they took her over to her granny's house. She called me and told me what he had done and where she was. I ran every red light to get to her. Even though I was way past mad, I used my head because it looked like I was the aggressor because I came over there, and the law is never good to me. But I called the police so they could meet me there. I had to play things this way because I wouldn't have been any good for her in jail for doing something to the punk for what he'd done to her. So, yeah, I did the right thing and called the police.

I had to call them again thirty minutes later when they didn't show up, and the fags still didn't come after that call. Hours passed with me sitting outside that house looking for the law to come help me. The respect and love I hold for my daughter's grandparents was the only reason I hadn't torn the walls off the bitch to get to beating that nigga's ass. He wouldn't come outside to me, not at first anyway. The punk called his people over there to help him with me. Remember, I was alone. All I saw was car after car pulling in behind the house. I swallowed my pride and called the police for the last time before calling Donna so she could come take Pooh home with her and come bail me outta jail when shit went down. Then I called my backup.

Donna was the first to pull up with two truckloads of females and her trusty 9 mm. Just before my niggas got there, Rick and his people came out of the house walking toward me talking shit. It was about eight of them. He must've thought I was a fool or something. There was no way I was finna try to fight him and all of them, but I wasn't a coward either. I took Donna's gun and fired a warning shot in the air. It made the smart ones run for cover and the rest stop in their tracks. At that moment, all types of cars, trucks, and vans got to pulling up, but also someone had called the police. They must've told them that it was two large groups of men outside with guns because they brought a SWAT team.

Everyone but Donna and her sister got the fuck outta Dodge. Peachee and Rick's bitch asses were talking to one of the officers while I underwent being searched as I tried to explain that I was the one who called in the first place. I couldn't believe it when I overheard that soft-ass punk telling the police that I was on paper, which I wasn't. My parole had ended almost a year ago. The crazy thing was I had half expected something like that to come from my ex, but to my surprise, she hadn't said much of nothing.

After a long song-and-dance with the police, I ended up walking away with my baby. Even though, they threatened to lock me up if anything was to happen to Rick. For the first time in my life they had come through for me. I had to take Pooh down to the station so photos could be taken of her bruises and we could give statements.

"Would you like to press charges, sir?" a tall cop asked, looking like he really wanted to put his big hands on somebody.

"All I want is my baby, and whatever report I need to have when I take her mother to court." Like I said, I'd deal with him in the streets.

I had to leave my daughter with Donna so I could meet up with my guys to make sure they all got away okay. I knew they were all strapped for war when I called and it wasn't gang-related either, for anyone who's thinking that way. Both Lords and Disciples came to my aid because the real recognize real, and loyalty is more than a flag.

So, fast forwarding like six months, I was in and

outta court for my daughter. I knew if I wanted to keep her with me I had to show the judge that I was more than the badass ex-con her mother was trying to make me out to be. So I dropped the divorce. How could I be good enough to take care of a child when I didn't have a stable home to put her in? Well, that's how I knew the courts would look at it when they found out about the divorce issue. It worked because the judge awarded me my baby, giving her mother two weekends a month for visiting. So that's how I ended up back in the house with Donna.

Things looked like they might be finally working out for me, but only time would tell.

Now Available Part 2

To order books, please fill out the order form below:
To order films please go to www.good2gofilms.com

Name:_____

Address:_____

City:_____State:_____Zip Code: _____

Phone:_____

Email:_____

Method of Payment: Check   VISA MASTERCARD

Credit Card#:_ _____

Name as it appears on card: _____

Signature: _____

Item Name	Price	Qty	Amount
48 Hours to Die – Silk White	$14.99		
A Hustler's Dream – Ernest Morris	$14.99		
A Hustler's Dream 2 – Ernest Morris	$14.99		
A Thug's Devotion – J. L. Rose and J. M. McMillon	$14.99		
All Eyes on Tommy Gunz – Warren Holloway	$14.99		
Black Reign – Ernest Morris	$14.99		
Bloody Mayhem Down South – Trayvon Jackson	$14.99		
Bloody Mayhem Down South 2 – Trayvon Jackson	$14.99		
Business Is Business – Silk White	$14.99		
Business Is Business 2 – Silk White	$14.99		
Business Is Business 3 – Silk White	$14.99		
Cash In Cash Out – Assa Raymond Baker	$14.99		
Cash In Cash Out 2 – Assa Raymond Baker	$14.99		
Childhood Sweethearts – Jacob Spears	$14.99		
Childhood Sweethearts 2 – Jacob Spears	$14.99		
Childhood Sweethearts 3 – Jacob Spears	$14.99		
Childhood Sweethearts 4 – Jacob Spears	$14.99		
Connected To The Plug – Dwan Marquis Williams	$14.99		
Connected To The Plug 2 – Dwan Marquis Williams	$14.99		
Connected To The Plug 3 – Dwan Williams	$14.99		
Cost of Betrayal – W.C. Holloway	$14.99		
Cost of Betrayal 2 – W.C. Holloway	$14.99		
Deadly Reunion – Ernest Morris	$14.99		
Dream's Life – Assa Raymond Baker	$14.99		
Flipping Numbers – Ernest Morris	$14.99		
Flipping Numbers 2 – Ernest Morris	$14.99		

Title	Price		
Forbidden Pleasure – Ernest Morris	$14.99		
He Loves Me, He Loves You Not – Mychea	$14.99		
He Loves Me, He Loves You Not 2 – Mychea	$14.99		
He Loves Me, He Loves You Not 3 – Mychea	$14.99		
He Loves Me, He Loves You Not 4 – Mychea	$14.99		
He Loves Me, He Loves You Not 5 – Mychea	$14.99		
Killing Signs – Ernest Morris	$14.99		
Killing Signs 2 – Ernest Morris	$14.99		
Kings of the Block – Dwan Willams	$14.99		
Kings of the Block 2 – Dwan Willams	$14.99		
Lord of My Land – Jay Morrison	$14.99		
Lost and Turned Out – Ernest Morris	$14.99		
Love & Dedication – W.C. Holloway	$14.99		
Love Hates Violence – De'Wayne Maris	$14.99		
Love Hates Violence 2 – De'Wayne Maris	$14.99		
Love Hates Violence 3 – De'Wayne Maris	$14.99		
Love Hates Violence 4 – De'Wayne Maris	$14.99		
Married To Da Streets – Silk White	$14.99		
M.E.R.C. – Make Every Rep Count Health and Fitness	$14.99		
Mercenary In Love – J.L. Rose & J.L. Turner	$14.99		
Money Make Me Cum – Ernest Morris	$14.99		
My Besties – Asia Hill	$14.99		
My Besties 2 – Asia Hill	$14.99		
My Besties 3 – Asia Hill	$14.99		
My Besties 4 – Asia Hill	$14.99		
My Boyfriend's Wife – Mychea	$14.99		
My Boyfriend's Wife 2 – Mychea	$14.99		
My Brothers Envy – J. L. Rose	$14.99		
My Brothers Envy 2 – J. L. Rose	$14.99		
Naughty Housewives – Ernest Morris	$14.99		
Naughty Housewives 2 – Ernest Morris	$14.99		
Naughty Housewives 3 – Ernest Morris	$14.99		
Naughty Housewives 4 – Ernest Morris	$14.99		
Never Be The Same – Silk White	$14.99		
Scarred Faces – Assa Raymond Baker	$14.99		

Scarred Knuckles – Assa Raymond Baker	$14.99		
Shades of Revenge – Assa Raymond Baker	$14.99		
Slumped – Jason Brent	$14.99		
Someone's Gonna Get It – Mychea	$14.99		
Stranded – Silk White	$14.99		
Supreme & Justice – Ernest Morris	$14.99		
Supreme & Justice 2 – Ernest Morris	$14.99		
Supreme & Justice 3 – Ernest Morris	$14.99		
Tears of a Hustler – Silk White	$14.99		
Tears of a Hustler 2 – Silk White	$14.99		
Tears of a Hustler 3 – Silk White	$14.99		
Tears of a Hustler 4 – Silk White	$14.99		
Tears of a Hustler 5 – Silk White	$14.99		
Tears of a Hustler 6 – Silk White	$14.99		
The Betrayal Within – Ernest Morris	$14.99		
The Last Love Letter – Warren Holloway	$14.99		
The Last Love Letter 2 – Warren Holloway	$14.99		
The Panty Ripper – Reality Way	$14.99		
The Panty Ripper 3 – Reality Way	$14.99		
The Solution – Jay Morrison	$14.99		
The Teflon Queen – Silk White	$14.99		
The Teflon Queen 2 – Silk White	$14.99		
The Teflon Queen 3 – Silk White	$14.99		
The Teflon Queen 4 – Silk White	$14.99		
The Teflon Queen 5 – Silk White	$14.99		
The Teflon Queen 6 – Silk White	$14.99		
The Vacation – Silk White	$14.99		
Tied To A Boss – J.L. Rose	$14.99		
Tied To A Boss 2 – J.L. Rose	$14.99		
Tied To A Boss 3 – J.L. Rose	$14.99		
Tied To A Boss 4 – J.L. Rose	$14.99		
Tied To A Boss 5 – J.L. Rose	$14.99		
Time Is Money – Silk White	$14.99		
Tomorrow's Not Promised – Robert Torres	$14.99		
Tomorrow's Not Promised 2 – Robert Torres	$14.99		
Two Mask One Heart – Jacob Spears and Trayvon Jackson	$14.99		

Two Mask One Heart 2 – Jacob Spears and Trayvon Jackson	$14.99		
Two Mask One Heart 3 – Jacob Spears and Trayvon Jackson	$14.99		
Wife – Assa Ray Baker & Raneissa Baker	$14.99		
Wife 2 – Assa Ray Baker & Raneissa Baker	$14.99		
Wrong Place Wrong Time – Silk White	$14.99		
Young Goonz – Reality Way	$14.99		
Subtotal:			
Tax:			
Shipping (Free) U.S. Media Mail:			
Total:			

Make Checks Payable To Good2Go Publishing, 7311 W Glass Lane, Laveen, AZ 85339

CPSIA information can be obtained
at www.ICGtesting.com
Printed in the USA
LVHW012008231120
672482LV00015B/2250

9 781947 340596